pB E

She reached across the void that separated them and touched him.

No wonder she had gone along with the hoax, wanting so desperately to believe him. She hadn't been willing to face the truth because she was falling in love with him.

"Can't you see what's happened between us?" Marc asked urgently.

"I'm only beginning to," she told him.

"And you do believe I love you?" he demanded.

Cathlyn couldn't answer. With all her being she wanted to trust him, and yet he had deceived her.

His fingers gripped her arm. "Cathlyn, you've got to believe me." His voice was raw with emotion. "How can I make you understand how much I love you?" And before she could even think of stopping him, he took her into his arms.

DECEIVE ME, DARLING

Barbara Siddon

Publisher's Note: This is a work of fiction. The characters, incidents, and dialogues are products of the author's imagination and are not to be construed as real. Any resemblance to actual events or persons, living or dead, is entirely coincidental.

PAGEANT BOOKS
225 Park Avenue South
New York, New York 10003

Cover artwork by Diana Voyajolu

Printed in the U.S.A.

First Pageant Books printing: July, 1988

10 9 8 7 6 5 4 3 2 1

To Lois, our most patient
proofreader and dedicated fan.

DECEIVE ME, DARLING

Chapter One

CHICAGO. CHRISTMAS DAY. Midway Airport was nearly deserted. As spiraling snowflakes bit her cheeks and clung to her long dark hair, Cathlyn Tate waded through the mounting drifts. The headlights of a lone taxi pierced the grayness. Gripping her suitcase tight in one hand and a canvas bag fat with presents in the other, she broke into a run.

"Taxi! Taxi!" she yelled into the icy wind, ducking her head and burying her chin in the collar of her red wool coat as she ran.

She caught only a glimpse of the tall, ski-jacketed figure racing toward the taxi from the opposite direction, before they collided head-on. The impact sent brightly wrapped presents skittering across a snowdrift, and Cathlyn felt herself teetering off-balance.

He caught her before she fell, wrapping one arm around her shoulders to steady her. "You should watch where you're going," he cautioned as he let her go.

"So should you," she fired back. Cathlyn scooped the presents into her shopping bag and grabbed her suitcase out of a snowbank. She flung herself, suitcase first, into the cab, only to feel the man pushing in beside her.

"You can't get in here," she protested.

"The hell I can't. This is the only cab within miles." He hauled in a suede duffel and slammed the door shut against the wind. "Where are you going?"

Cathlyn looked at him carefully. He was slender, with very broad shoulders, and had thick dark hair that fell across his forehead. His fine-honed features gave him an almost aristocratic appearance. There was an unmistakable self-assurance about him and a defiance in the set of his jaw that told her he wasn't about to give up the cab. She might as well answer his question. "The lakefront, Near North," she replied briskly. "And I'm in a hurry."

"That's on my way," he announced, sounding no more pleased with the situation than she was. "In the spirit of Christmas, I'll drop you off first."

"Now, you wait just a minute. This is my cab!" she replied.

His hazel eyes appraised her. "Correction," he said, smiling slightly, "this is our cab, and we might as well share it civilly."

"You two gonna sit back there and argue, or

you goin' somewhere?" the driver interjected from the front seat. "I ain't got all day."

"Just off Fullerton, near the Drive," Cathlyn directed coolly. The driver grunted acknowledgment.

"Would you like me to help you brush the snow off your packages before it melts through?" her companion asked amiably as the taxi crept along the snow-packed road.

Cathlyn glanced down at the presents in her bag. "I suppose that would be a good idea."

His eyes met hers, and she didn't look away. It was as though they'd declared a silent truce. The tension between them seemed to diminish.

"By the way, I'm Marc Harrison," he offered, reaching for one of the packages.

Cathlyn assessed the man sitting beside her. He was athletic-looking, four or five years older than she was—maybe thirty-five—with a dimple right in the middle of a very square, firm chin. Droplets of melting snow dotted the shock of hair that fell across his forehead.

"I'm Cathlyn Tate," she finally told him.

"Merry Christmas, Cathlyn," he replied. "Let's get rid of this snow before your entire bag turns into a puddle."

Cathlyn nodded, her lips moving in the beginning of a smile.

They removed the presents one by one and tapped them against the seat to knock off the snow. "You're going to make somebody happy today with all these," he observed. "Are you on your way home to see your family?"

Cathlyn tensed. Family implied something she

hadn't been a part of for years. "Yes and no," she answered. "I spent Christmas Eve in Detroit with my sister. Now I'm going to stop by my apartment before I have Christmas dinner—stop!" She took a red-and-green striped package from his hand. "That breaks," she cautioned.

"What is it?" he asked.

"A crystal angel. It's blown glass with lacy wings like a snowflake."

Marc watched her carefully while she described the angel, the lilt of her voice painting pictures of something delicate and graceful, very much, he thought, like herself. She moved her hands as she talked, dusting away the snow. Her eyes were cornflower-blue, almost gentle now that her anger had dissipated.

"What were you doing at the airport on Christmas?" she asked, fixing those eyes on him.

"Just got back from Aspen," he told her. "Have you ever skied there?"

"Not recently." That was part of the life she'd walked away from.

"Too bad," he remarked.

She'd never thought so and still didn't. "Are you going home?" she asked him.

He grinned. "I'm going to put in an appearance at the traditional family dinner, if that's what you mean."

"It sounds as if you'd rather be skiing."

"Well, we do what we have to do," he said with a shrug. He turned back the cuff of his jacket to check a sleek, black sports watch. "At this rate I'm going to be damned late." He tapped on the sliding glass window above the front seat to get the driver's attention. "There must be a faster way to do this," he said when the cabbie opened the glass.

"Not unless you got a snowmobile, buddy," answered the cabbie sourly. "You looked out the window recently?"

Marc and Cathlyn simultaneously looked out at the swirling snow that shrouded the cab in white. "How about Lake Shore Drive?" Marc asked patiently.

"Closed 'cause of drifts." The cabbie snorted, stroking a two-day growth of beard.

"The expressway?"

"Can't get up the ramps. Too slick." Just in front of them a traffic light turned red and the driver touched the brakes. In slow motion the cab slid sideways into the empty intersection. "Told the wife this morning she shoulda bought me those chains for these tires," he grumbled. "Guess we'll try the shortcut. My brother, Joe, he drives a plow. He always keeps that street clear."

Cathlyn frowned. She had expected to be home within the hour, but she didn't feel hopeful. She would certainly be late for dinner, if she made it at all. Marc Harrison seemed to be in as much of a hurry as she was. Although he didn't sound very enthusiastic about where he was going, he was obviously anxious to get there.

The cab turned down a side street, proceeding slowly between the rows of parked cars already disappearing under mounds of snow. Christmas trees lit the front windows of the symmetrical brick row houses. Glancing sideways, Cathlyn noticed that she and Marc were both sitting toward the center of the seat where they had moved to reach the Christmas presents. She sensed that she should move, but she felt no desire to pull away.

Marc didn't seem to be paying any attention. "At this rate we'll be lucky to get there by the New Year," he noted loudly enough for the cabbie to hear.

The driver honked impatiently at a group of carolers, loudly singing "Jingle Bells" as they walked hand in hand down the middle of the street. "Got any better ideas?" he called back.

"I do," Cathlyn interrupted suddenly. "Take us to the subway."

"The subway?" Marc tried to remember the last time he'd ridden the train.

"Anything you say, lady," the cabbie agreed. "But it's a ways to the station."

"Maybe we'd be better off with the cab," Marc hedged. "Are you sure the trains run on Christmas?"

"Of course. They run every day. Don't you live here?"

"All my life." He shrugged. "That doesn't necessarily make me intimately familiar with the CTA."

How odd, Cathlyn thought, to live in Chicago and not ride the CTA. She looked at him curiously. But that was his problem. Tonight the train would be the fastest way home. "Do what you like," she said, checking her watch. "You can drop me at the subway."

Marc hesitated. Something fascinated him about this dark-haired woman in the red coat.

Even though he knew practically nothing about her, he found himself reluctant to leave her. Maybe he'd play along for a while, just to see what happened. Even if it meant riding the CTA.

"Are you really in that much of a hurry?" he asked her.

Cathlyn found herself wondering whether she really was. But she had promised, and she was already late. Maybe he'd change his mind about riding the train when they got to the station. "I guess I'm just impatient to get home," she answered slowly. "It's Christmas, remember? And it's slipping away."

They rode in silence while the cab inched past a strip of neighborhood shops, skidding at every stop sign. The driver muttered intermittently about his wife and the tire chains and the weather in Chicago. Cathlyn hoped he knew where he was going, because she had no idea. She was beginning to be glad she wasn't alone in the cab.

Without warning, a snowmobile flashed in front of them, and the cabbie slammed on the brakes and hit the horn. Marc grabbed for Cathlyn, holding tight to her as the taxi spun through an icy intersection, finally coming to rest in a snowdrift.

"Are you all right?" Marc asked.

Quickly Cathlyn pulled back, aware that her head had been buried against his chest. Instinctively she had gone to him, and he had made her feel secure. Trembling slightly, she drew in a sharp breath. Only then did he release his grip on her arms, leaving her with the ghost of his touch through her heavy coat.

"I'm fine, I think," she answered slowly. She didn't add that she was shaking inside, and she wasn't sure her reaction had been caused by the careening cab. "What happened?" she asked in a dazed voice.

"Smart-aleck snow jockey." The cabbie snarled and leapt out of the cab to survey the situation.

Marc opened his door to look out, and a cold blast of wind heavy with snow rushed in. The back wheels of the cab were buried deep in a drift.

"We're stuck," announced the driver, poking his head back inside.

"I gathered," Cathlyn responded dryly. "So what do we do now?"

"I push," Marc determined.

The men got out of the cab and Cathlyn followed, stepping in drifts nearly to the tops of her black leather boots, but neither Marc nor the cabbie seemed at all interested in either her advice or her offers of help.

"Lady," the cabbie finally said in an exasperated voice, "best thing you can do is get back in the cab and weigh down the back end." She didn't argue, glad to be out of the fiercely blowing snow. The two men worked for nearly half an hour, digging around the wheels with an old coffee can and then rocking the cab back and forth with one pushing and the other at the steering wheel. The tires spun, but the cab, which was on an angle with its rear end down against the curb, didn't move.

Cathlyn was still sitting in the backseat, tapping her foot and trying to come up with an alternative solution, when the cab belched several puffs of sooty smoke from under the hood. The driver gestured angrily. She saw Marc hurry around the cab to inspect the damage and was tempted to join him but thought better of it.

Marc's nose and cheeks were scarlet, and his hair was caked with snow when he finally opened Cathlyn's door. "Come on," he said, "we're not going anywhere in this taxi. The clutch is gone."

Cathlyn stared at him, realizing they were no longer strangers. It was funny, she thought, how circumstances sometimes did that to people. "Then we need to figure out something else really fast," she pointed out, getting out of the cab. "It's Christmas."

"Sterling observation," he noted. "You got any ideas?"

"Not at the moment," she admitted, surveying the silent street. The storm had subsided somewhat, and the wind had died, leaving huge, fluffy snowflakes, drifting lazily down.

"Hurry up," Marc urged, already several steps ahead of her.

But Cathlyn was caught up in the scene around her. The white mantle had worked a quiet magic on the old neighborhood, with its tattered awnings and iron gates across the closed shop doors. Christmas lights twinkled along the storefronts, and frazzled green Christmas wreaths were laden with snow.

"Wait," she called out. "Have you looked around? It's beautiful."

Marc stopped and turned, staring at her. Snowflakes were caught in her hair, and her cheeks were pink from the cold. As she came closer, he could see her blue eyes glistening in the light from the streetlights breaking the early dusk. She moved gracefully through the snow. There was an air about her that reminded him of a lovely snow queen.

"Yes, beautiful," he agreed, never taking his eyes off Cathlyn.

The way he looked at her made Cathlyn strangely uncomfortable. "So where are we going?" she asked.

He wanted to brush the snowflake off her nose. "Over there." He motioned to a lighted storefront about halfway down the block. "The cabbie says he knows somebody."

The snow-covered street was deserted as they slowly approached the frosted glass door where the cabbie had disappeared. A fluorescent pink neon sign reading DAWN'S DINER flashed on and off in the adjacent window. Cathlyn looked at the faded poinsettia drooped across the windowsill. "We're going in here?" she questioned.

"That's what the man said." Marc shoved the door open for her, and they stepped inside.

Smells of grease, plastic, day-old coffee, and pine-scented floor wax all blended together. A radio blared out Perry Como's version of "White Christmas." Cathlyn surveyed the handful of people huddled at the counter on stools rising like chrome-based mushrooms out of the floor, and then glanced quickly at a few other patrons scattered around the speckled, plastic-topped tables.

"This is where we're spending Christmas?" she whispered. Her eyes followed the silver tinsel garlands that had been painstakingly stretched from four ceiling lights to the top of a plastic Christmas tree elevated on a table in the center of the room.

Marc was still looking around. "Not on your life," he assured her.

"Hey, babe, how ya doin'," the driver was saying to an ample blond woman who leaned over the counter to hug him. Cathlyn assumed she was Dawn.

"Merry Christmas," the blonde shouted boisterously. "Your brother, Joe, said he'd be in later. Who's this you brought with you?" She nodded at Marc and Cathlyn, who were still standing near the door.

"Oh, them." The driver momentarily appeared to have forgotten. "They're a fare. I got hung up in a damn drift. Clutch burned out."

"So you're all gonna spend Christmas with us." Dawn beamed. "Hey, Millie, put on some more coffee," she yelled over her shoulder, then turned back toward Marc and Cathlyn. "Sit down," she urged, gesturing toward a table. "The more the merrier."

"I thought you said we weren't going to spend Christmas here," Cathlyn whispered to Marc.

Reluctantly she followed him to a table in the corner, away from the one Dawn had indicated.

"I'm thinking, I'm thinking," he retorted. "I suppose we might as well take off our coats." He walked around the table to help slip her coat off her shoulders. As it fell back across the chair, his hands brushed the soft fabric of her red silk dress, sending an unexpected tremor of warmth through her. She wondered whether his hands had lingered intentionally or whether it had been her imagination.

She watched him return to his chair, pulling off his own jacket as he walked. She couldn't quite figure out this man, or what it was about him that stirred such fascination in her. Coming back alone from a holiday ski trip in Aspen to have dinner with his family probably meant he wasn't married. His clothes, his manners, his general demeanor all hinted at wealth and power. She'd known plenty of men like that while she was growing up—men like her father. She'd left that world behind long ago.

But Marc didn't affect her that way. Maybe it was because she liked him, she thought ruefully. His name did have a familiar ring, although she was certain she'd never met him before. He wasn't someone she'd have forgotten. I wonder who he is? she thought curiously. Probably the best approach was to ask him. On the other hand, if she waited, maybe he'd tell her more about himself. People often did.

"You hungry?" he asked abruptly.

Cathlyn hadn't really thought about it. "Not particularly," she answered.

"Well, I am." He looked at his watch again. "I'm supposed to be sitting down to dinner right now. They're probably wondering where the hell I am."

"You could call," she suggested. "That's what I'm planning to do."

"After I order," he said firmly. "You go make your phone call, and I'll get us something to eat."

Cathlyn walked across the restaurant and pumped money into the pay phone. She jiggled the receiver and ultimately pounded on the phone case with her fist. She got nothing but static on the line.

"Easy on the phone," Dawn bellowed across the diner, and several heads turned toward Cathlyn. "You ain't gonna get through on there even if you beat it to death. Phone's not workin'."

Grudgingly Cathlyn gave up.

"No luck, huh?" Marc said when she returned to the table.

"We might as well be marooned on a desert island," Cathlyn noted glumly.

"Then we'd have to settle for coconuts and fish. Here we can have turkey with gravy, stuffing, mashed potatoes, and slaw on the side."

"You didn't!" she exclaimed. The radio began playing "White Christmas" for the third time since their arrival.

"Why not?" he asked good-naturedly. "It's Christmas."

The coffee, which Dawn generously announced was on the house, turned out to be as black as tar, but Cathlyn found herself hungrily eating the turkey and stuffing.

"You told me you've been at your sister's," Marc said between bites. "Do your parents live here?"

There wasn't any reason to explain about her parents, Cathlyn decided. "No, I came home to spend Christmas with some friends," she answered. "Did you ever hear of Angel House?"

Marc quickly took another bite of turkey. "Angel House?" he repeated, stalling for time. What was her connection with Angel House?

"It's a place out on the West Side that takes in homeless girls, a halfway house, sort of," she began, her eyes lighting with enthusiasm as she talked. "It belongs to my friend Jean Monahan and her husband, Tommy."

That explained it. Marc kept eating. He considered telling her that they had a common interest, one of those odd coincidences that sometimes come up when you meet a stranger. But he usually didn't discuss his charitable contributions. He let his tax accountant take care of them, trying to remain as much in the background as possible. Maybe he'd wait. "So what does Angel House have to do with your Christmas?" he asked her.

"I promised to spend the day with them, and have dinner and play the guitar while we all sing Christmas carols tonight in front of the fire," she told him between forkfuls of mashed potatoes. "Christmas is the hardest day of all for kids who aren't with their own families."

He tried to envision this woman in red sitting cross-legged in front of the fire playing her guitar for a bunch of homeless girls. She was different from any of the other women he knew. He'd almost told her that he knew all about Angel House, but he didn't. What he knew was the balance sheet. He decided not to bring it up. "And that's why you're in so much of a hurry—because you want to get to Angel House?" he asked curiously.

"Can you think of a better reason?" she asked. "They're counting on me."

"I guess I can't," he acknowledged.

Cathlyn looked up to see that Marc's plate was as empty as hers. "That dinner really wasn't too bad," she admitted. "I envisioned pressed turkey floating in grease."

Marc conjured up a horrified expression. "At Dawn's Diner? Never!"

"Oh, ye of great faith," Cathlyn quipped.

"Now, about getting out of here," Marc said, wiping his mouth with his napkin. "My brother's got a four-wheel-drive. He's up at my parents, but he'd probably be willing to come get us."

"And just how are you going to communicate with him?" Cathlyn looked amused. "By carrier pigeon?"

"That's right." Marc frowned. "The phones are out."

"Got ya some fresh coffee," Dawn broke in, appearing with the pot.

"How far is it to the subway station?" Cathlyn asked.

"Maybe two miles," Dawn estimated. "But you ain't gonna make it walking, if that's what you got in mind. Temperature's hit ten degrees and still goin' down. Your toes would drop off in those boots."

As if to make the point, the door to the diner burst open, admitting a blast of frigid air. A brawny man in a red-and-black lumberjack coat stamped snow off his boots.

"Hey, Joe, ya made it," Dawn and the cabbie shouted almost in unison.

The big man called out jovial greetings to nearly everyone in the place. He glanced curiously at Marc and Cathlyn.

"You workin' today, Joe?" Dawn asked him.

"Yeah," he confirmed. "Really lousy out there. Drifts up to your eyeballs. Ya got any of your special coffee?"

"Just the way you like it, Joe." Dawn winked at him.

Cathlyn watched the steaming cup disappear entirely in his huge hands. "Do you suppose that's the cabbie's brother?" she asked Marc.

"Looks that way," he replied. "Isn't he the one who drives the plow?"

"Maybe. Hey, wait a minute," Cathlyn exclaimed. Their eyes met, the germ of an idea formulating simultaneously. "If he drives a plow, and he got here, that means he's got one of the only things moving . . ."

"Then he's our ticket out of here," Marc finished.

Cathlyn leaned forward, ready for action. "Do you ask him or do I?"

"We wait." Marc settled back in his chair. "First we let him drink that 'special coffee,' which will no doubt warm him up substantially.

Then we decide whether to appeal to his wallet or his Christmas spirit."

"Or maybe his brother," Cathlyn reasoned. "He's the one who got us in this mess in the first place."

"You may have a point." Marc gave her a searching look. Rarely did people around him come up with options he hadn't already considered.

They waited about twenty minutes while Joe ate two bowls of chili and joked with Dawn. Cathlyn looked around, pondering the people who would voluntarily spend Christmas in a diner, but most of all she puzzled about the man in the deep blue Norwegian ski sweater who sat across the table from her. As a psychologist, she knew a lot about people, enough to know he was different, but she wasn't sure why. She and Marc Harrison both wanted to be somewhere else on this special day, and yet she felt comfortable with him in this little neighborhood diner eating Christmas dinner and listening to the carols blaring from the radio.

She studied his tousled hair where the snow had melted and dried, and noticed that his cheeks were still reddened from the wind. The angular lines of his sun-bronzed face reflected the strength and assurance of a powerful man. She saw the hint of a smile when his eyes caught hers, and found herself much less anxious to leave than she had been at first.

"Your name sounds familiar," she began conversationally. "Should I recognize it?"

"Don't know any reason why you should," he

answered quickly. Suddenly he didn't want to tell her who he was. He had the distinct impression that his money and his life-style would get in the way.

"What field are you in?" she pursued.

"I'm, er, in construction."

She waited, expecting him to elaborate.

"Do you want some dessert?" he asked instead. "Dawn said they have homemade pumpkin pie."

"No, I don't think so." She suspected he was evading her question, but she wasn't sure.

"Then let me see what I can do with Joe." Abruptly he stood up, scraping his chair across the worn wood floor. He sauntered easily toward the counter. He could be in construction, she mused; he certainly had the build for it. The broad shoulders, the trim waist, the lithe grace about him.

He approached Joe and the cabbie from behind, clapping the cabbie on the back in one of those male greetings. She caught a glimpse of Marc's profile and saw both men warm to his engaging grin. Soon he had struck up a conversation, and all three were laughing. Maybe he's a salesman, she thought, selling construction supplies. That didn't fit, either.

Suddenly both Joe and the cabbie glanced in her direction, and she quickly produced a glowing smile. They nodded knowingly and Marc kept talking. What, she wondered, was going on? At least he appeared to be making progress. That was the critical thing. She saw him reach for his wallet and extract two bills. He handed one to each man. They nodded, smiled some more, and stuffed the money into their pockets. Victory, she thought.

Marc had an impish grin on his face when he came back.

"You did it?" she asked.

"Right you are," he announced smugly.

"But it took more than an appeal to the Christmas spirit, right?"

"It took our entire arsenal," he said, laughing. He paused, giving her a thoughtful look. "There are a couple of things you probably should know before we leave," he added.

"Like what?" Cathlyn asked. Something in his tone made her wary.

He glanced at the check Dawn had left on the table and again reached for his wallet. "Like I told them, we'd eloped last night and were on our way to make the happy announcement to our families."

Cathlyn stared at him. "You did what?"

"I told them it was the only opportunity we'd have with everyone together. And besides that, if we got there too late, we'd have to spend the night and sleep right out in the open on the roll-away bed."

Now she understood those looks the men had exchanged. "You can't tell them something like that," she protested.

"Why not?" he inquired innocently. "It worked." He slipped a bill under the edge of his plate and pulled on his jacket.

"That's outrageous!" Cathlyn stood up, her eyes dancing as she thought about the story he'd concocted. "How much is the check? I'll pay for mine," she announced, not waiting for him to help her with her coat.

"My treat today." He chuckled. "What kind of a man would let his new bride buy her own Christmas dinner?"

"Cut it out," she fired back, trying to keep the laughter out of her voice. She started for the door, but he stopped her, his hand firm on her arm. She turned and found herself standing very close to him. He smelled good, crisp and masculine.

"There is one other thing you should know."

"What now? What other preposterous story could you possibly have told them?" She was choking back laughter as she questioned him.

"It's not what I told them," he began. "It's about this snowplow we're going to ride."

"Yes?" She braced herself.

"It's a converted garbage truck."

"A garbage truck?" She must have misunderstood.

"Right. It was the best I could do on short notice." Still holding her arm, he guided her toward the door. "Come on, let's get our things out of the taxi."

Their ticket to freedom was parked directly outside the door. Cathlyn stared at the huge hulk of a truck that had been designed to chew up mountains of trash. An angular plow blade had been attached to the front, which was the custom in Chicago whenever the snow exceeded the capacity of the regular plows.

"Christmas Day in a garbage truck," she commented to no one in particular. "When my sister told me to have a wonderful day, I'm not sure this is what she had in mind."

"Told you we weren't going to spend Christmas in the diner," Marc reminded her, "at least not all of it."

"Maybe I should have inquired about the alternatives," she said, following him to the snowbound taxi.

The wind had increased again, a harsh wind out of the north, but the snow had stopped almost entirely. Cathlyn gathered up the presents, which didn't look much the worse for their bout with the snowdrift, and put them back into her canvas bag. Marc lifted out her suitcase, carrying it in the same hand with his duffel. The street was slick where the plow had scraped away the top layers of snow, exposing icy patches underneath. They had walked only a few steps when Marc took her hand. It was a motion that seemed perfectly natural, yet Cathlyn found herself thinking of nothing else as they walked along the snow-packed street. She was almost surprised to find Joe and the cabbie waiting for them by the truck.

"We're all going in here?" Cathlyn queried, looking up at the tiny cab in the front of the garbage truck.

"Yep," confirmed the cabbie.

"How will we all fit?" she asked, trying to envision four people, their luggage, and a bag of Christmas presents squeezed into the cramped cab.

Joe gave his brother a knowing wink. "Well, little lady," he said, swinging himself up, "might be tight normally, but under the circumstances . . ." The cabbie snorted, and Marc grinned innocuously.

"All right, mister," Joe said, directing Marc, "you hand up the stuff and then climb up here. We'll bring the lady up last."

Cathlyn watched apprehensively as Marc pulled himself up the high step and disappeared inside the front of the garbage truck. She shivered in the icy wind. Dawn was right, the temperature must be down below zero. Her toes and fingers were freezing, and she longed for her fur hat. At least the truck didn't smell. She'd always thought garbage trucks probably did. Maybe even the smells were frozen.

"Your turn, lady," Joe said from behind her, and Cathlyn felt his massive hands around her waist hoisting her up like a bag of feathers into Marc's waiting arms.

Cold and uncomfortable, she felt herself being wedged into the cab, her knees against the metal dashboard and the door handle poking into her back. Marc's legs were firm beneath her. His chest was tight against her shoulder. The warmth of his breath brushed her cheek, and his presence surrounded her.

"You fit real nice there on his lap." The cabbie winked as Cathlyn settled back against Marc.

"Are you comfortable?" Marc asked her.

"Well, not exactly," she admitted, wiggling sideways. Marc slipped his arm around her waist and let his hand rest lightly against her leg. A tremulous sensation crept through her, momentarily blotting out everything else.

Joe pulled himself easily into the driver's seat and made a remark under his breath that produced a loud guffaw from the cabbie.

"How long is this ride going to take?" Cathlyn inquired.

"Maybe twenty minutes," Joe surmised, starting the truck. "Depends on how much plowin' we do on the way."

"Couldn't you plow after you drop us off?" she shouted over the roaring engine.

"You ain't tellin' me you don't like it there?" Joe chortled. "You just make yourself right at home, little lady. Don't pay no attention to us." He yanked hard on a black handle that dropped the plow, and immediately a spray of snow fanned toward the curb. The cabbie coughed loudly, stealing a sideways glance at them.

Cathlyn could feel Marc shaking with laughter. He seemed to be enjoying the whole thing. Well, she decided, if they all thought it was so amusing, maybe she could do them one better. She wiggled again to extricate her knees from the knife-edged cold of the dashboard.

"What an enchanting way to spend our first Christmas together," she murmured to Marc in a voice loud enough for everyone to hear even over the scraping of the plow blade. "Let me get just a little closer." She wrapped her arms around his neck and nuzzled close to his cheek. If she was going to be cast as the blushing bride, then she'd see just how much he liked the role of the enamored bridegroom.

Marc cleared his throat. She felt him tense, and his body shifted beneath her. "Why, darling, you're shivering," he said, the silvery tone of his voice exaggerating his words. "Let me keep you warm."

She was aware of every inch of him as he snuggled her into the curve of his lap. Her cheek rubbed his chin, which was rough against her tender skin. It wasn't the reaction she'd expected from Marc, or from herself. Cathlyn started to pull back but could move only far enough to bury her nose in Marc's soft, curly hair. Tingling inside, she plunged on. "Maybe we should just ride around all evening plowing the South Side of Chicago. It's such a lovely view from way up here." Her voice got more syrupy as she threw herself into the role.

"Oh, no, love, because when I get you home—" Marc stopped, the note of suggestiveness in his voice producing snickers from both Joe and the cabbie.

Knowing he had the better of her, Cathlyn decided it was time to change the subject. The warmth of his body, beneath her and all around her, seeped through her coat, enveloping her. She had to find a diversion. "Maybe we should sing carols while we ride," she suggested.

Marc stared at her as though she had lost her mind, but Joe laughed raucously. "I always go for a cold shower myself," he cracked, before blasting out "Jingle Bells" in a deep bass voice.

One by one they joined in, Marc's rich baritone, her soft soprano, and Joe's slightly off-key tenor blending in a lusty harmony, punctuated by the scraping of the plow. The louder they sang, the faster Joe drove, bouncing them up and down harder and harder as the truck picked up speed.

"No one would ever believe this," she whispered to Marc between songs. "It's the craziest Christmas I've ever spent."

He nodded agreement, aware that for some inexplicable reason he was having fun. A world away, in the big Colonial house in Winnetka, his family was gathered around the Chippendale table, sipping vintage wine from sparkling crystal and no doubt discussing the recent dip in the stock market. He was riding around the South Side in a garbage truck and liking every minute of it. He savored Cathlyn's warmth against him. It probably wouldn't be necessary to mention this particular escapade to his father.

"Stop!" Cathlyn called out suddenly, right in the middle of "Frosty the Snowman." The truck lurched to a halt.

"That's the subway station," she announced, pointing to the lighted overhead sign.

"Right you are, little lady," Joe confirmed. "Sure you don't want to take a run down Halsted Street?"

"Not tonight," Marc told him firmly.

"Oh, yeah," Joe recalled, "you got that problem with the rollaway bed." Laughing heartily, he and the cabbie exchanged a knowing look. The truck emitted a series of loud beeps as Joe backed it past a snowdrift to bring them closer to the curb. When he took their things and then helped them down, Marc and Cathlyn moved slowly, their muscles tight and sore after the cramped ride.

"Merry Christmas!" yelled the cabbie, waving furiously as the truck pulled away. "Hope you make it in time."

Both Marc and Cathlyn waved back before picking up their belongings from the snow.

"I don't believe you got us into that," Cathlyn said, shaking her head.

"Me?" he shot back. "I'm the one who got us out of that. You're the one who wanted to ride around singing Christmas carols in a garbage truck."

They stared at each other until the absurdity of the situation overtook them and they burst into gales of laughter. Marc leaned forward quickly, his lips warm against the cold of her cheek as they brushed her ever so lightly. His touch filled her like the silent magic of Christmas, and for a moment neither of them moved. Then Marc gently took her arm. "Come on," he said. "We've got a train to catch."

Together they raced down the subway stairs and fumbled for change, their fingers almost too cold to put the money in the turnstiles. A nearly empty train was just pulling into the station when they reached the platform, and they hurried through the sliding doors to collapse in the nearest seat. Cathlyn found herself sitting very close to Marc as they talked and laughed about Joe and the cabbie and Dawn's Diner. They were downtown before either of them realized it.

"This is my stop," Cathlyn blurted out suddenly when the train rolled slowly into the station. The doors were opening as she grabbed her suitcase in one hand and the bag of presents in the other.

"Wait!" Marc reached for his duffel, which was stuck under the seat.

"I can't," she called back, leaping through doors already beginning to close.

He jerked the duffel free, but the train had begun to move. "Cathlyn! Stop! Your last name—" he cried out. He caught one last glimpse of her on the station platform before the train was engulfed in the darkness of the tunnel. Agitated and alone in the subway car, he paced back and forth. "Cathlyn, Cathlyn . . ." he repeated over and over, hoping that somehow her last name would come to him. When it didn't, he sat down again and stared glumly at the lights streaking by the window. Maybe he could find her, anyway, or maybe it was one of those strange interludes that is best committed to memory and left alone. Shrugging his shoulders, he decided to ride the train to Howard Street. His brother could come down from Winnetka in the four-wheel-drive. Maybe the family had at least saved him some dessert.

Cathlyn watched the train until it was swallowed up by the tunnel and the last sounds were gone. Then she gathered her belongings and walked slowly up the stairs. She would probably never see Marc Harrison again, but she'd never forget this Christmas. She knew already that an evening at Angel House, which was to have been the highlight of her day, would be an anticlimax.

The gusty wind, which hit her full in the face when she emerged from the subway, was sweeping the powdery snow into ever-increasing drifts. She walked briskly along Lincoln Park West with thoughts of Marc flicking in and out. In the stillness, with only the wind for company, she was acutely aware of being alone.

Chapter Two

❖❖❖

MARC HARRISON SHOVED open the massive oak door of the renovated brownstone that served as the offices for Harrison Associates, Inc.

"Good morning, Ms. James," he called out to his secretary as he closed his umbrella and strode into his outer office.

A slinky blond woman with red-lacquered nails appeared from behind a screen of tropical plants. "Good morning, Mr. Harrison," she cooed. "Your mail and the newspapers are on your desk." Nodding a brief acknowledgment, Marc kept on walking toward his private office.

"And you have an appointment with your brother in fifteen minutes," Ms. James called after him.

Marc hung his camel-colored cashmere overcoat in his closet, along with his umbrella, and settled himself behind his mahogany conference desk. He began to rifle through the morning mail.

"Nothing much here," he muttered to himself. "It's as dismal as the weather." He glanced out the bay window and watched the rain run in rivulets down the outside of the leaded glass. March is a lousy month in Chicago, he thought to himself. A clap of thunder crashed, and lightning ripped across the sky. Marc's intercom buzzed.

"Yes, Ms. James," he answered.

"Be sure to look at the business section of the morning newspaper today, sir." The secretary's voice sounded hollow and electronic. "There is an article about one of the Harrison projects—that complex of boutiques that's opening next week."

The intercom clicked off, and Marc pulled the business section from the inside of the newspaper. As he skimmed through it, a picture of a group of psychologists who had published a study on stress and business executives caught his eye. There was something vaguely familiar about the attractive woman—the only woman—in the center of several austere-looking men. Maybe it was the long dark hair. Quickly Marc scanned the picture's caption until he found the name he was looking for. "Dr. Cathlyn Tate, vice-president of the Windy City Psychologists Association. . . ."

"Well, I'll be damned," Marc uttered aloud. A broad grin spread across his face. He never would have guessed that ethereal creature with the big blue eyes was a shrink.

"Come in," he called in response to a loud

knock at the door. As his brother's tall frame appeared in the doorway, Marc boomed out, "Wait until you see this, Andy." Folded newspaper in hand, Marc crossed the Oriental carpet in a few long strides. "Here's a picture of that woman I told you about, the one in the red coat."

Andrew Harrison stashed his umbrella in the brass stand and shook the rain from his trench coat. "You mean your Christmas angel from the taxi?" he asked.

"That's the one," Marc confirmed. He thrust the newspaper into his brother's hand. "Take a look at her. Isn't she something?"

Andrew squinted at the newspaper photo and then let out a low, appreciative whistle. "Very nice," he agreed. "Do I sense another female in your future?"

"Maybe so," Marc answered nonchalantly. Impulsively he sat down and punched his intercom button. "Ms. James, get me the phone number for Dr. Cathlyn Tate. Try the Windy City Psychologists Association."

"She doesn't look like your type," Andrew commented, settling himself on a wooden chair in front of Marc's desk.

"What do you mean, 'my type'?" Marc bristled.

"I can't quite fathom an eminent psychologist hooking up with a playboy-artist," Andrew remarked.

"Architect," Marc corrected with a flare in his eyes. "Just because I didn't follow the Harrison's well-worn path to Harvard Law School like you—" The intercom buzzed again, and Marc scrawled a phone number on his memo pad. "Got it!" he exclaimed, waving the piece of paper triumphantly under his brother's nose.

Andrew appeared unimpressed. "Unless, of course, she decides to go after your money," he continued, as though Marc had never spoken. "Like the last one. What was her name, anyway? That one was a real gold digger."

"Quit playing brother's keeper," Marc said without hostility. He grinned at the picture again. "This woman is different."

"They're all different." Andrew shrugged.

"I don't think this woman is impressed with money," Marc declared.

"Every woman is impressed with money," Andrew argued. "Some just have a higher price."

"You're jaded," Marc told him. "But I'm going to operate a little differently with this one," he added thoughtfully. "She doesn't know a damned thing about me, and there's no reason I have to tell her until I get to know her better. I'll play it low-key for a little while—"

"You? Low-key?" Andrew laughed. "That's hardly your style. If you couldn't take one of your lady loves to the brink on the second date and to bed by the third, you wouldn't know what to do."

"You've been watching too many X-rated movies," Marc retorted, and then leaned forward impatiently. "Let's get this McKinley contract out of the way. I've got an important phone call to make."

* * *

Several blocks away, Cathlyn Tate pushed open the heavy glass door of her office on the twenty-seventh floor of the Hartford Building.

"Good morning, Shirley," she called out to her secretary as she peeled off her blue all-weather coat and tossed it on a chrome rack in the corner of the waiting room.

A short, plump woman in a snug-fitting suit opened the sliding glass panel in front of the reception desk. "Thank goodness you're here, Dr. Tate," she exclaimed, leaning through the opening. "Your phone has been ringing off the hook all morning, and your first patient is due any moment, and there have been two cancellations and three add-ons—"

While Shirley paused to catch her breath, Cathlyn reached through the open panel and picked up a fistful of yellow phone messages. "You're doing just fine," she said soothingly, patting her secretary on the arm. "I can tell everything's under control."

"Well, it won't stay that way if you don't return those phone calls first thing," Shirley warned. "Mr. Tompkins's wife said he's very depressed again, and Mrs. Bixby wants to bring in her daughter for a joint session, and the Psychologists Association called—"

"I'll take care of it, I'll take care of it," promised Cathlyn. She breezed into her office, dropping the phone messages on top of the mountain of folders and paper on her teakwood desk. She snapped the black vertical blinds open, clearing them entirely away from the window. Seeing that her usual panoramic view was lost in the pouring rain, she rolled a sleek, white-cushioned chair toward the concave edge of her curved desk and sat down with her back to the window. She barely had begun to sort the messages when a shrill ring pierced her concentration. Damn, she thought. I forgot to turn off the phone last night.

It rang again. "I've got it, Shirley," she called to her secretary. "You can finish watering the plants." She grabbed the receiver. "Family Therapy Center, Dr. Tate speaking," she answered in a brisk, businesslike voice.

"Dr. Tate? Cathlyn Tate?" questioned the cool, masculine voice on the other end. "Marc Harrison here," he continued, not waiting for a reply.

"Marc Harrison?" Instantly she knew. Her voice softened as she answered, "Yes, this is Cathlyn."

"I saw your picture in the newspaper this morning," he explained.

So that was why he'd called after all this time. "Wait a minute, I haven't seen it yet," she replied.

"Section D, page twelve," he said. Quickly Cathlyn dug around on her desk until she found the paper. She'd almost expected to hear from him in those first few days, but after New Year's came and went, and the days melted into weeks, she'd dismissed the possibility. She thumbed through the business section until she located page twelve. Dreadful, she thought with a grimace. How could he ever have recognized me from this?

"I didn't know you were a psychologist," he commented, "and such a noted one."

"The business reporter liked our study," she replied. "He said he'd always suspected prominent businessmen had problems of their own."

Marc laughed. "I could have told him that without having to do any studies. But the reason I'm calling," he continued, "is that I'd like to take you to lunch today."

Cathlyn hesitated only long enough to make sure her calendar was clear. "I'd like that," she responded warmly. "I'm in the Hartford Building."

"I know," Marc said. "I'll pick you up at eleven-thirty." His words were followed by a click, and then a buzzing tone on the line.

Well, well, she mused, tapping her pencil on the edge of the desk. How interesting. "Shirley," she called. "Block out eleven-thirty to two on my appointment sheet. I've got a lunch date."

Instantly Shirley appeared at the door of Cathlyn's office. "With whom?" she demanded.

"Boy, are you nosy. You sound like my mother. But for your information, it's with a man named Marc Harrison and . . ."

"You mean that guy from the garbage truck?" Shirley's eyebrows flew up in surprise.

"That's the one." Cathlyn smiled. The memory flooded her with warm, happy feelings.

Shirley shook her head. "You'd better be careful," she warned. "He sounds like some kind of nut. Anyone who would spend Christmas Day riding around on a garbage truck . . ."

"I spent my Christmas that way," Cathlyn observed. "Does that make me some kind of a nut?"

Shirley opened her mouth to reply, but Cathlyn held up her hand. "Never mind answering that."

The door to the outer office opened, and Shirley scurried back to her desk, muttering under her breath.

Cathlyn reached for the file on her first patient. Alexandra Bixby, age seventy-four. Suspected senility. Referred by her daughter, who is alarmed because she sings to her canary, talks to the philodendron, and fills her entire freezer with home-baked bread. It had often occurred to Cathlyn that if the daughter would spend a little time with her mother, Mrs. Bixby would have someone to talk to besides the plants and would probably make cookies for the grandchildren instead of baking bread for the birds. But the daughter still insisted on counseling sessions.

Three hours later Cathlyn was drained. No one had ever warned her that being a psychologist was such an emotionally demanding job.

She was jotting her impressions in her last patient's record when Shirley appeared at the office door.

"Dr. Tate?"

"Is it important?" Cathlyn didn't look up from her work. "I want to finish this before I go to lunch."

"She said it's knee-deep already. . . ."

Out of the corner of her eye Cathlyn could see her secretary jiggling nervously from one foot to the other. With a sigh she put down her pen. "Yes?"

"She's afraid if it keeps raining like this, it will come right up the stairs and flood the whole place, and she doesn't know what she's going to do about the girls, and Tom's out of town. She was in a real panic."

"Shirley!" Cathlyn stopped her. "Begin at the beginning."

"That friend of yours, Jean Monahan from Angel House—"

"Jean?" The problem suddenly took on a different dimension. After years of dealing with adolescent girls, Jean could take almost anything in stride.

"She says the sump pump's out and water is pouring into the basement." Shirley talked faster and faster. "She wants all the buckets she can get her hands on, and when the kids start coming home from school, she's going to start a bucket brigade and dump the water out that window on the high side of the basement before it gets into the furnace room."

Cathlyn was on her feet, reaching for her coat by the time her secretary paused for a breath.

"Call her back and tell her I'm on the way," she directed, then glanced at the clock. Marc was due in a few minutes. An image of him as she had seen him last, in his ski jacket in the snow, smiling down at her as he took her hand, clouded her resolve but only briefly. As much as she wanted to go with Marc, she had an obligation to Jean. How do you tell a friend with an emergency that you're sorry, but you have a lunch date?

"You'll have to give Marc Harrison my regrets," she instructed Shirley reluctantly.

"But Dr. Tate, you wanted to see him," Shirley protested. "Maybe I could take the buckets to Angel House."

"Explain to Mr. Harrison that I had a crisis and apologize for me," Cathlyn continued rapidly. "How's the rest of the afternoon?"

"Except for the lunch you're not having," Shirley began in a tone that made it clear she thought Cathlyn was missing a golden opportunity, "you're free. You're supposed to be updating computer files."

"Block out some time for that later in the week." Cathlyn grabbed her fold-up umbrella and slung her purse over her shoulder. "And take off early if you want," she called back as she flew past the open door of the outer office, her total energy suddenly focused on Angel House and how she could help Jean Monahan solve her problem. The bucket brigade sounded like a reasonable idea, assuming they could come up with the buckets, but only as a stopgap. It was still raining torrents. Ultimately they needed to prevent the water from coming in. And if they could find someone to fix the pump . . . Her mind stirred ideas, weighing one against another as she sought the most pragmatic approach.

"Hey!" A strong hand gripped her arm, forcing her to an abrupt stop. "Where are you going in such a hurry?"

"What?" Cathlyn's gaze traveled upward to meet Marc Harrison's deep hazel eyes.

"If I had known you were in such a rush to eat, I'd have picked you up earlier." He smiled down at her.

Cathlyn stared at the unexpected apparition. The eyes, the firm cut of his jaw, the tiniest hint of a dimple when he smiled—those were just the same as she remembered. But he seemed taller, more commanding, than before. He was dressed impeccably. His open topcoat revealed the edges of a dark brown suit, crisp white shirt, and a silk tie in muted earth tones. He already had folded his black umbrella into a cylinder about a foot long, which he carried in his left hand.

"Marc Harrison, remember? We're going to lunch."

"Oh." Cathlyn drew her breath in hard. "But you're early."

"As a matter of fact," he corrected her, "I am precisely on time."

"My secretary was going to explain," she began. "I can't go. Something has come up." What had seemed a compelling problem a few minutes before now seemed trivial as she stood face-to-face with him. It would have been lots easier to tell him why she was backing out of their date if he hadn't been standing there, still holding her arm.

"What do you mean 'something has come up'?" His eyes narrowed ever so slightly, making his displeasure readily apparent.

"It's an emergency. That's why I couldn't let you know," Cathlyn continued quickly. "A friend of mine called a few minutes ago. Her basement is flooding, her husband is out of town, and she's terribly worried about the furnace and how to keep the house warm enough for all the children tonight." Realizing that she was blithering on like her secretary, Cathlyn abruptly applied the brakes. "I'll have to take a rain check on lunch," she finished more calmly. "I need to go help her."

"Just exactly what do you anticipate doing to solve her problem?" he inquired, his eyes twinkling with amusement. "I suppose you plan to carry out the washer and dryer on your back and build a dike around the furnace."

Even though he was making fun of her, there was no malice in his voice, and she couldn't help but laugh at his ludicrous image. "Actually, Jean had an outstanding idea," she announced proudly. "I'm going to buy some buckets, and when the girls come home, we're going to form a bucket brigade."

Now it was his turn to laugh. "Like a coffee can to bail out a rowboat?" He shook his head at her. "Unless your friend lives in a trailer, it's going to take more than that." He gripped her arm firmly. "Come on," he muttered with resignation, "let's see what we can do."

"We?" Cathlyn echoed. "What a marvelous idea!" She started impatiently toward the elevator. "I'll drive. My car is in the downstairs lot."

"Not so fast," Marc murmured into her hair in the midst of the crowded elevator. "Lunch first."

"We can grab a hamburger on the way," Cathlyn tossed out breezily as the elevator doors opened to the lobby.

"We'll do no such thing," Marc declared.

Cathlyn turned toward him in dismay. "The basement is flooded, the water is rising, and you want to go to lunch?"

Something told him she wouldn't give in. "Tell you what," he compromised. "There's a deli down the street with pretty good corned beef on rye."

She gave him a broad smile. "Perfect!" she exclaimed. He let her go ahead of him through the revolving door. "I'll pick you up under the awning," she said as they came out.

"You want kosher pickles with yours?" he yelled after her as she took off at full speed through the rain.

"Of course," she called back over her shoulder.

When Cathlyn reappeared, honking loudly from behind the wheel of her yellow Toyota, Mark was waiting, sheltering their food under his coat. He watched her weave the little car deftly through traffic. When he'd invited her to lunch, this was hardly the scenario he'd had in mind. Right about now the maître d' at The Whaler should have been ushering them to a select table for two near the tall windows overlooking the river. They'd have chatted casually over a glass of wine and moved into more serious conversation while they ate their way slowly through a magnificent preordered lunch, served course by course. By the time they reached the raspberries and cream, Marc would have been in a position to determine whether this relationship was worth pursuing. Whatever his decision, Cathlyn would have come away never having seen a menu, and unless she was familiar with the restaurant, which he doubted, she would have been unaware of the prices, which even he thought were steep.

It had been a masterful plan, except for the fact that it hadn't worked. Instead, he was standing in the rain, clutching a deli bag to his chest and hoping the pickles wouldn't leak through on his suit, waiting to cram his body into a tiny thing hardly worthy of being called an automobile, to drive off to some godforsaken place and slog through a flooded basement. She'd better be worth it, he thought with a sigh, and strode resolutely into the rain.

After twenty minutes in the Toyota, Marc felt nearly as cramped as he had riding in the garbage truck. "Is this place much farther?" he inquired, looking out the window in hopes of spotting someplace he could buy dessert.

Cathlyn took the last bite of her pickle and brushed the bread crumbs off her green linen dress. "Only a few more blocks," she reassured him. She glanced at him, wondering whether bringing him along had been a smart move. This could take the rest of the day, and he had only invited her to have lunch. She was doing a good deed because a close friend needed her, but where did that leave Marc? He'd never even met the Monahans. She hadn't exactly invited him, she thought, consoling herself silently. He had announced he was coming. Still, he probably didn't have any idea what he was getting into.

They wound down a narrow street lined with big old homes, many of which had seen better days. Marc looked out the window at the seedy frame houses with their overgrown shrubbery and cracked sidewalks. "Interesting neighborhood," he noted. "Is your friend into real-estate investment?"

"Hardly," Cathlyn responded. "Her only investment is in people." She slowed down and honked at a large black dog that ambled down the middle of the street. "By the way," she said, "you told me you're in construction; do you work on renovating old houses like these?"

"Sometimes," Marc answered vaguely.

"What else do you do?" Cathlyn pressed. "When I think of construction, I think of somebody in a hard hat with a hammer in his hand. You don't fit that image."

"Are you trying to tell me I don't look as if I know which end of a hammer to pound with?" Marc adopted a pained expression.

"I see. You don't like to talk about your job," Cathlyn responded.

"You're working overtime, lady psychologist," Marc warned.

Cathlyn's ears burned, and she didn't answer. It was probably the most common complaint everyone in the profession got from family and friends. All the other cracks about being a shrink rolled off. But she was still sensitive when people took what she considered normal understanding and recast it as cold professionalism.

"Hey"—he reached over and took her arm— "I

didn't mean that. I was just teasing you. I didn't realize it would hurt."

"It didn't," she answered brightly.

"You don't lie very well," he remonstrated. "Lack of practice, probably."

Cathlyn touched the brakes and expertly maneuvered the car into an almost nonexistent parking place.

"Pretty slick," he noted. "That you're good at."

He put his hand on her arm again. The light pressure of his fingers burned into her flesh. She turned toward him, again seeing the glint of green in his hazel eyes as he appraised her. "I don't know you very well yet," he said seriously. "I don't know the 'Dr. Tate' part of you at all, and I admit that I've got some preconceptions about psychologists."

"You and most of the rest of the world," she said with a sigh. "It's because people are afraid psychologists can see parts of them they don't want to expose."

Marc stared at her. How much had she figured out about him? "What an odd analysis," he mused. "I wonder if you're right."

"Of course I'm right," she answered smugly. "Now, just one favor—believe me when I tell you that I don't have any magic powers." She kept her voice light. "If you ever want to see Dr. Tate, make an appointment and come to the office. Otherwise, let me just be Cathlyn."

He took both her hands, and warmth spread from where he touched her. The world around them was silent, except for the rain beating in a heavy staccato on the metal roof of the car and running in sheets down the windows. She suddenly felt very close to him, aware of his mouth, the crinkle lines along his eyes, the tilt of his head.

His voice was husky when he spoke to her. "We all seem to carry around a lot of excess baggage because of who or what we are. You just be Cathlyn Tate, the beautiful lady in the red coat, and I'll be Marc Harrison, the guy you shared the taxi with. And we'll see where we go from here. A deal?"

His hands tightened on hers, and instinctively she knew he was conveying something important. She didn't know what or why, but deep down she sensed that in these moments in the rain, they had said more to each other than either of them had expected.

"It's a deal," she agreed.

For a moment he didn't move. Then he leaned toward her ever so slightly, and Cathlyn had the crazy feeling he was going to kiss her. But if that was what he'd intended, he changed his mind. "Now," he said decisively, "let's go take a look at this flooded basement."

Chapter Three

MARC OPENED HIS car door slightly and peered out through the rain. "This is it?"

He surveyed a frame monstrosity with peeling paint and a lopsided porch that stretched across the entire front of the structure, tilting at the corner where it wrapped around and disappeared. "This is where your friend lives?" he asked in disbelief.

"Yep, this is it," Cathlyn confirmed. "It looks better when the sun's out."

"It appears to need some work," Marc noted cautiously. "Is that wooden figure hovering over the front door some sort of Art Deco thing or what?"

Cathlyn reached for her purse and her umbrella, then opened her car door. "That's not Art Deco at all," she informed him. "That wonderful hand-carved angel is the symbol for Angel House."

Angel House! She hadn't told him they were going to Angel House. He looked it over more carefully. So this was the place he was helping to support. Then another thought occurred to him. What if someone in there recognized his name? He wasn't ready to tell Cathlyn any more about Marc Harrison than she already knew.

"Are you coming or not?" Cathlyn stuck her head through the open car door. "It's raining out here, in case you hadn't noticed."

"Just getting my umbrella," Marc muttered. Resolutely he shoved the car door wide open and stepped out into the driving rain. Cathlyn tiptoed around the back of the car, balancing carefully so her high heels wouldn't get stuck in the mud. "Let's run," he yelled, grabbing her free hand.

She dashed up the sidewalk behind him, trying to avoid the largest puddles. They dropped their umbrellas and scraped their feet hard on the rough rubber welcome mat before pushing open the heavy front door, which stood slightly ajar.

"Jean . . . hello, Jean?" Cathlyn called into the dim, cavernous hallway. "It's me, Cathlyn. Jean, where are you?" The words echoed back at her. Then a petite young woman with a headful of coal-black curls and a face dwarfed behind huge tortoiseshell glasses popped into view.

"Cathlyn, thank God you're here! I've called everyone I can think of, and absolutely no one's available, and Tom's at the conference in Colorado . . ."

While her friend rambled on excitedly, Cathlyn slipped out of her wet coat and hung it on one of the bent hooks that was screwed into the wall. Several of the other hooks were littered with a scruffy assortment of scarves, hats, and jackets.

Jean stopped her monologue abruptly, eyeing Marc. "We don't seem to have met," she observed.

"Sorry," Cathlyn said apologetically. "This is Marc—"

"Nice to meet you," Marc interrupted, extending his hand warmly toward Jean before

Cathlyn could finish introducing him. "I understand you're having a problem with your basement."

"A problem—that has to be the understatement of the week," Jean exclaimed. "Did you bring any buckets?" she asked Cathlyn.

"No," Cathlyn admitted. "Marc said unless you lived in a trailer, that wouldn't work."

"So what's your brilliant idea?" Jean challenged Marc.

He shifted uncomfortably, not expecting her to zero in on him. At least she didn't seem to recognize him. She wouldn't be so blunt with Marc Harrison, philanthropist.

"Listen," Marc suggested, "why don't I call in a crew of workmen—I know some guys from my job—and you could have a new sump pump installed in no time flat. That would alleviate the water problem for the moment, and then when things dry out, you could have a study done—"

"You can't be serious," Jean cut in, her eyes like saucers behind her glasses. "Cathlyn must not have told you much about Angel House. It takes two basic commodities to operate this place—love and money. Love we've got; money's as scarce as snowballs in July." She looked toward Cathlyn, shaking her head in frustration. "You should have brought the buckets," she said.

"Well, then . . ." Marc's hand gravitated toward his inside suit-coat pocket. His basic inclination was to solve the problem with his checkbook. It would be a simple matter to make a few phone calls, get a crew in to replace the pump and do whatever else was needed, and then simply write a check for the whole job. Maybe he could take Cathlyn to dinner instead of lunch. He glanced downward to find those deep blue eyes fixed expectantly on him. He withdrew his hand. Nope, buddy, no checks this time, he decided silently. You're just plain old Marc Harrison, remember?

"In that case, let's get busy," he said with resignation. He stripped off his suit jacket and dropped it in line next to Cathlyn's coat on the row of hooks. "I think I know where I can come up with an only slightly used sump pump, cheap. I'll install it myself."

"Really?" Jean looked him over apprehensively. "Do you know how?"

"He's in construction," Cathlyn ventured, realizing Marc didn't look much like somebody who'd know a sump pump from a road grader.

"He is? How handy!" Jean exclaimed, suddenly warming to him. "Let's get you some clothes. And some boots. Tom's got waders he uses for fishing in the fall. . . ." Her voice trailed off as she disappeared behind the stairs, taking Marc with her.

When they reappeared, Marc had an odd collection of clothes slung over his arm, including an enormous pair of yellow rubber boots that Cathlyn assumed were the waders. "All you need now is your fishing pole," she told him, "and you can go out and catch a trout for dinner."

"Don't knock it," Marc retorted, loosening his tie and unbuttoning the top button on his shirt. "Fishing—particularly trout fishing—is an honorable undertaking." As he talked, he removed his tie altogether and continued unbuttoning his shirt. Cathlyn was suddenly aware of his crisp, dark hair curling up at the open neck. He stopped directly in front of her, and she took a tiny step back. There was no longer any question of who was in charge.

"Maybe we'll go fishing together sometime," he remarked casually. "But right now," he continued, "you need to quit being decorative and go call the fire department and get them busy pumping out that basement."

"Will they do that?" Cathlyn asked skeptically.

"It depends entirely on how you handle it." He grinned. "If you ask them, probably not. But if you tell them a convincing story about all the poor orphaned children who will be without shelter tonight because the Board of Health is going to condemn their home for unsanitary conditions, you should get pretty fast action."

"Yes, sir, on the double," Cathlyn called after him as he went up the stairs to change his clothes. She laughed to herself. He could kid her all he wanted about her job, but he was no slouch, either, when it came to figuring out how to get things done. In fact, he thought the same way she did: Define the problem, consider the options, pick one, and go for it. And she was willing to bet he didn't come up empty-handed very often. Cathlyn thought back to his uncharacteristic interruption when she had introduced him to Jean. He hadn't even given her a chance to say his last name before he'd cut in. In retrospect, he'd bordered on rude. But the moment had passed so quickly that it probably wasn't worth making an issue out of it.

"You're not dressed for this occasion, either," Jean observed, coming back to the hall. Cathlyn nodded agreement as she looked down at her deep green linen dress and camel pumps. "Come on," Jean said, starting up the stairs. "With eighteen females in the house, there's got to be something up here that will fit you."

While she changed, Cathlyn considered how to approach the firemen. She knew it was not city policy to pump out private basements, and she suspected Marc figured it was really a long shot, even if he didn't present it that way. She felt herself rising to his challenge. This was one time when she really wanted to succeed, no matter what kind of outrageous story she had to come up with.

When Cathlyn bounced down the basement stairs a short time later, she wore a pair of Nikes, some snugly fitting white denims, an even more snugly fitting red T-shirt, and a victorious smile. Staring into the dimness, she saw a splash of yellow color across the expanse of muddy water. "The firemen are on their way," she called out triumphantly, stopping just above the water line.

"You're kidding." Marc sounded surprised. "They're not really coming."

"Don't act so amazed. You're the one who said it would work."

"You *are* serious!" He sloshed over to her through the water. "Just exactly what did you tell them?"

"Oh, well, I just sort of explained the situation," she answered vaguely.

"Ah, yes"—Marc gestured dramatically—"nothing tugs at a man's heartstrings quite so hard as the sounds of a damsel in distress—and every damsel knows it."

"Cut that out before I push you in headfirst," she threatened. She gave him a shove, and he teetered precariously on the stair before he grabbed for her, very nearly sending them both tumbling into the dirty water. For a moment neither of them moved. Both his arms were around her, enclosing her in a circle with her head against his chest. She relaxed against him, and his breath, as warm as the summer sun, grazed her cheek. His chin was rough with traces of an afternoon beard as she rubbed her forehead along the line of his jaw, liking the sensation. After a moment he lifted his head, but he still held her to him tightly, and she didn't try to push away.

"We both might have ended up swimming, you know," he told her.

"I know," she answered sheepishly, looking at the murky water. "But we didn't." Marc took off his work gloves. She felt his fingers slip gently beneath her long, dark curls, and rested her head lightly in the hollow of his shoulder.

"I'm never sure what you're going to do next," he murmured into her hair. Very slowly he drew back and looked at her. "That's quite a shirt you're wearing, lady," he noted. His eyes caressed her, and she pulled back, knowing she hadn't actually been touched but feeling as if she had.

"You're sort of classy, yourself," she answered softly, letting her eyes travel up the yellow waders to the red-checked flannel shirt with its sleeves rolled up above his muscular forearms. She smiled at the streak of dirt on his cheek, and the unruly shock of hair flopped across his forehead.

Almost self-consciously, he rubbed his forehead across his shirt sleeve. "I'm probably pretty grubby," he said. "I had to unhook the gas lines to get those dryers up there with the washers." He pointed to several mismatched washers and dryers piled on some mahogany tables in the center of the basement. "Both freezers seem all right so far. They're on the high end of the slope in the floor. But we need to get this water out of here. When do you think those firemen are going to show up?"

As if in answer to his question, a burly firemen stomped down the stairs behind Cathlyn and soon was calling to the others outside, who opened basement windows and snaked their hoses through. Cathlyn watched, fascinated, as the water began to recede almost immediately.

"Hey, how come there's a fire truck in front of the house?" a distant female voice demanded.

Cathlyn heard a rumbling, like elephants charging through the front hall. "School bus is here," Jean announced unnecessarily from the hallway.

"What's on fire? Is my boom box safe?" demanded another voice.

Cathlyn walked up the basement stairs to watch a dozen or more adolescent females milling around Jean, who was alternately reassuring them and stirring them into action. "Carmelita!" Jean's voice rose over the chattering din. "You're on hall detail this week—get the mop before someone slips in the puddles."

"Okay"—the olive-skinned Hispanic girl grinned—"but not if the house is on fire. If we're going to burn down, it's dumb to mop first."

"You are absolutely correct," Cathlyn interjected. "Except we're not burning, we're flooding. The firemen are pumping water out of the basement."

"Yo, Cathlyn," called out a tiny blond girl. Scattered cheers arose as several of the others spotted Cathlyn.

"Hey, Cathlyn, did you bring your guitar? Let's sing that song about Noah building an ark," the girl proposed.

Cathlyn laughed. "Not right now, Sondra."

"Hey, don't bug her," called out another. "Can't you see she's busy making time with her boyfriend?"

"How did you ever guess?" Cathlyn answered easily, looking over her shoulder to find Marc standing behind her, surveying the confusion. "My elegant ensemble must have given me away," she continued, gliding forward, placing one hand on her hip and whirling around in an imitation of a high-fashion model. Her performance was met by a round of applause from the girls and a big grin from Marc.

He must think I'm really strange, thought

Cathlyn. When she considered the situation objectively, it was really silly. Well, she decided, this is the way I am, and he can take it or leave it. She stole another glance at Marc and found him leaning casually against the wall, his eyes following her with obvious fascination. He had taken off the waders, leaving him barefoot in a pair of Tom's jeans, which were skintight on him. The streak of dirt was gone from his cheek, but his hair still flopped in his eyes. As he stood there, eating an apple someone apparently had thrust into his hand, he looked to Cathlyn a little like an overgrown Huck Finn. What a pair we must make, she thought, working hard to suppress an attack of the giggles.

"All right, ladies, the show is over." Jean's voice pierced the noise. "Anyone who doesn't have after-school chores, head for the basement. The water's pretty much gone, and Mr. umm . . ." Jean paused, staring briefly at Marc. "And Marc has used bandages and chewing gum to get the sump pump going temporarily. But the mop-up needs an army, and we're it. Right face, march," she commanded in her mock drill sergeant's voice, turning on her heel toward the basement stairs.

Amid laughter and good-natured grumbling, the group began to disperse. Marc walked up behind Cathlyn and put his hand lightly on her shoulder. "She's really good with them," he observed, clearly impressed. "She's tough, but not heavy-handed about it. They obviously respect her."

"She cares about them, and they know it," Cathlyn replied thoughtfully.

A rather plump girl, lagging behind the others, stalked past Marc and Cathlyn, muttering loudly, "Dinner is probably going to be really late."

"We may not get around to dinner at all tonight, Mandy," Cathlyn warned in an ominous voice.

"Really?" Mandy stopped and gave Cathlyn a stricken look.

"Don't worry," Marc reassured her. "Some people around here may not get hungry," he continued pointedly, "but the rest of us do. There will be food." Looking relieved, Mandy disappeared through the basement door. "Now that I've climbed out on a limb, just exactly how does dinner work around here?" Marc asked Cathlyn.

"I thought you were being a little rash," she jested. "Jean posts the menus and the kitchen work schedule on a bulletin board inside the pantry. We can take a look and see what's planned for tonight."

She led Marc into a barn of a kitchen with an enormous rectangular table running down the center. Opening a small door in the far corner, she stepped inside the pantry.

Marc followed her. "This is a snug fit," he commented, squeezing between the floor-to-ceiling shelves, stacked to capacity with an eclectic mixture of pots, pans, dishes, and glassware. Had it not been for a streetlight that glowed through a tiny window at the far end, the room would have been pitch-black.

Cathlyn wiggled around a wooden drying rack overflowing with dish towels, and fumbled for the light she knew was there somewhere. "Darn, I can't find it," she exclaimed. "There's a chain—it hangs from a single bulb in the ceiling," she told Marc. "Do you see it?"

"Over here, maybe?" he suggested. He stepped forward and, in the close confines of the pantry, bumped hard into Cathlyn.

"Are you all right?" he asked, gripping her shoulders.

Marc's fingers seared through the light fabric of the skimpy cotton T-shirt as though Cathlyn had been wearing nothing at all. As she reached out to steady herself, her hands closed over the crisp, curly hair of his forearms. His muscles were taut and firm against her palms.

He drew her closer. "I didn't mean to do you in," he whispered.

"I'm okay," she reassured him in a strange, throaty voice she hardly recognized as her own. His aura settled around her like a curtain against the rest of the world. He had a rich, musky, very male smell. She felt the rhythmic cadence of his heart and the deep, steady pulse of his breathing. But most of all she felt him, warm and strong against her.

His arms tightened around her and she reached upward, sliding her hands across the soft flannel of his shirt toward his shoulders. When she tipped her head back, she saw his silhouette in the dim light before his mouth covered hers. Although his lips were gentle, she felt the ancient power that flows between a man and a woman building deep within her. Lost in the seclusion of his arms, Cathlyn floated on waves of pleasure. Her lips softened against his mouth, and she moved with him, sharing and exploring. When they parted, it was slowly, reluctantly. With the magic of those moments still clinging to them, she nestled her head against his shoulder.

"Cathlyn," Marc whispered hoarsely into her tousled hair.

"Yes?" she answered, almost unwilling to speak because she knew words would break the spell.

"We came in here to check the menu for tonight's dinner." His voice was clearer now, but his arms still encircled her.

"But I couldn't reach the light chain," she reminded him, making no move to pull away.

"That's right," Marc answered. Slowly he released her. She could feel his reluctance as if it were a tangible thing. The kiss they had shared had been almost mystical, and even when they weren't touching, its unseen bond remained. She heard a soft click, and the tiny room was immersed in the harsh light from the bare bulb hanging from the ceiling.

"I sure wind up in some strange places with you." Marc grinned down at her.

She didn't need a mirror to be aware of the warm flush high on her cheekbones. "Just think what you'd have missed in life if it hadn't been for me," she said jokingly. "A garbage truck, a flooded basement, the Angel House pantry, to say nothing of Dawn's Diner. And to think I barely know you."

He took her arm with an abruptness that stopped her. His voice was almost rough. "Is that how you feel, that we barely know each other?"

"No," she replied, suddenly serious. "It's a funny thing, Marc. I realize I don't know you, or anything about you, but it doesn't seem that way. It seems . . ." She paused, with nowhere left to go. She didn't know how it seemed, except that it was very special.

"It seems that we've always known each other," he finished for her. "Is that what you were trying to say?"

"I guess so. I don't know," she answered honestly. "Do you feel like that?"

"Yes, Cathlyn, like I've known you forever." His words hung in the silence between them for several moments. Then Marc grinned and playfully tousled her hair. "Now, where was it you said Jean posts that menu?" he asked, looking around.

"Right here." Cathlyn turned toward the bulletin board and ran her finger down Jean's meal plan. She could still feel Marc standing close behind her.

"Looks like tonight's selection is beef stew with dumplings. That takes hours," he noted, checking his watch.

"True," Cathlyn agreed. "But maybe if we get going and use a lot of tenderizer on the meat, we can speed it up. The girls who cook tonight are all down in the basement working, so it looks as if we're the kitchen detail."

"Us? Make stew for twenty people?" He gulped.

"Just the same as making stew for two, except you make ten times as much," Cathlyn observed pragmatically. "You get that bag of potatoes and I'll look for the meat."

Cathlyn was opening the refrigerator door when Jean bounded into the kitchen. "There you are," she exclaimed. "I've been looking for you. The fireman you talked to on the phone is ready to leave, and he wants to meet you before he goes."

"Right now?" Cathlyn asked.

"He said something about being curious about that lady who rescued the girl who hid inside the dryer because she was afraid of being swept away by the flood," Jean explained.

"Whoops," Cathlyn said under her breath. When she had told that story, she'd never expected to have to confront the person behind that anonymous voice on the phone.

"The lady who what?" Marc questioned as he appeared with a ten-pound bag of potatoes in his hand.

"Never mind," Cathlyn answered. "I have to go meet a fireman. I'll send you some help from downstairs."

"I'm certainly glad someone's doing something about dinner," Jean called back to Marc as they left the kitchen. "The tenderizer is on top of the refrigerator."

Marc looked helplessly from the bag of potatoes in his hand to the giant economy-size can of tenderizer on top of the refrigerator. He made outstanding crepes suzette and Cherries Jubilee. But stew? For twenty? He set the potatoes on the floor. Perching on a tall stool with a torn plastic seat, he let his eyes travel from the cracked linoleum floor down the length of the marred wood table to the old black six-burner stove that anchored one end of the chipped countertop.

His stomach rumbled, reminding him of his promise that there would be food. Suddenly he stood up and put the potatoes back in the pantry. He might not be equal to stew for twenty, but he certainly could produce something for them to eat. Returning to the kitchen, he reached for the telephone.

Thirty minutes later there was a loud pounding on the front door.

"Somebody get that," Jean yelled from the basement. Several girls materialized in the front hall, and one of them flung open the door.

"Luigi's Pizza—delivery," announced a gruff voice.

"We didn't order any pizza," the surprised girl protested.

"Somebody at this address did," declared the deliveryman as he stepped inside. He placed a precarious stack of flat, white pizza cartons on the hall table, balanced his crooked red umbrella on top of them, and fished in his back pocket for the order. Drawn by the noise and the tantalizing smell of the pizza, more girls filtered into the hall.

"Eight large pizzas—four cheese and four pepperoni—and a case of soda," he read aloud. "Comes to $87.48. Cash only." Someone gasped.

"I ordered those," Marc announced, striding out from the kitchen. He reached into his wallet and pulled out two fifty-dollar bills. "Keep the change," he muttered, stuffing the bills into the deliveryman's outstretched hand. "It's a rotten night."

"Gee, thanks, buddy." The deliveryman looked surprised. "The soda's on the porch. I'll get it right away."

Marc turned to the knot of stunned, silent girls behind him. "Isn't anyone hungry?"

Tentatively a few heads nodded.

"Then what are you waiting for?" Marc boomed. "Let's get these pizzas to the kitchen and sound the dinner gong."

Cathlyn stood quietly in the shadows at the rear of the hallway watching the girls carry the pizzas to the kitchen. Something about Marc Harrison just didn't add up. He had just forked over one hundred dollars for pizza, including a tip so big that even the deliveryman had been surprised. Yet he hadn't been flashy about it. In fact, he'd seemed almost embarrassed.

Meticulously she examined what little information she had. Marc had told her he worked in construction, and judging from the way he slogged around the basement and dealt with the broken sump pump, the trade was obviously familiar to him. That was really all she knew. He'd made it pretty obvious he didn't want to discuss his work.

Cathlyn idly picked up Marc's suit coat, which someone had rescued from its hook and laid carefully over the back of a chair. She turned it inside out, but the standard label was missing. In fact, there wasn't a label of any kind in the lining. Carefully she ran her fingers over the soft roll of the collar, examining the fine handwork. She rubbed the fabric between her fingers, noticing that although it appeared to be the finest of wool, it wasn't wrinkled even after being thrown around on a rainy day. Unless she missed her guess, this was a custom-made suit of extraordinary quality. Why would someone who worked in construction have his suits custom-made? Maybe he owned the construction company. Or was difficult to fit off the rack. Or both.

Cathlyn laid the jacket back on the chair, carefully smoothing it out. It simply didn't add up, and despite all her expertise in figuring out people, she didn't know why.

"Hey, Cathlyn, come and eat," one of the girls shouted from the kitchen. "We're waiting for you."

Quickly she joined the noisy, chaotic group in the kitchen. The table was strewn with open pizza boxes, and the girls were poised, ready to strike. Everyone talked at once. They'd never seen so much carry-out pizza all in one place at one time, and cans of soda were definitely a first for dinner at Angel House. It was like a party, one noted. Another said she hoped the basement flooded on a regular basis if this was part of it. Cathlyn was quiet, watching Marc fit into the group and field the girls' incessant questions as though he ate dinner with seventeen adolescent females every day of his life.

Jean nudged Cathlyn under the table. "Come on, let's go get the rest of the sodas."

"But couldn't one of the girls—"

"Come on," Jean said, cutting her off.

When they reached the front hall, Jean continued. "How well do you know Marc . . . Marc, what's his last name?"

"Harrison," Cathlyn told her friend. "Not very well. He's the one I met at Christmas."

"Oh, he's the one from Dawn's Diner," Jean remembered. "Didn't you tell me when you came in that he's in construction?"

"That's what he said." Cathlyn nodded.

"Take a look at his hands, especially those short, immaculate nails," Jean pointed out. "And listen to the way he talks, his vocabulary. This guy is polished. He has class."

Cathlyn wished her friend weren't quite so observant. "Look," she said, "you're not telling me anything I haven't already wondered about. We both know he didn't exactly crawl out from under a rock."

Jean laughed lightly. "There's something about his name too. It seems to me I've heard it somewhere before, but I can't quite place it. Of course, you know me, I'm lousy at names."

"Harrison is a common last name"—Cathlyn shrugged as they headed back into the kitchen—"and Marc is hardly unusual, either." They sat down and Cathlyn returned Marc's smile from the other end of the table. When he turned back to his young audience, she studied his well-balanced features and the firm line of his jaw. Something was gnawing at the edge of her consciousness, a vague feeling, but there nonetheless.

"Well," said Jean, crumpling up her napkin, "don't rush into anything until you have a few more pieces of pizza."

"Don't worry about me." Cathlyn laughed. "My genetic heritage includes a big dose of good old Midwestern common sense."

"It does?" Marc inquired dryly, walking up behind her. "Why haven't I seen any signs of it?"

"Maybe you just haven't recognized it when you've seen it," Cathlyn responded. "What, for example, would be the most logical thing for us to do right now?"

"Well . . ." Marc began expansively.

Recognizing that her foot was poised, ready to insert in her mouth, Cathlyn hurried on. "The absolutely crystal-clear, obvious answer at this moment—with the basement under control, dinner over, and no dishes to wash—is a guitar and a roaring fire in the fireplace and lots of voices blending in song."

"It is?" Marc asked.

"It is," Cathlyn proclaimed. "If you'll provide the fire, I'll get my guitar out of the car," she offered. "And I know exactly where we can find the voices." Marc groaned.

"Anyone who wants to join me for folk songs in front of the fireplace, be in the living room in ten minutes," she announced in a loud voice. Remembering Marc's blasé attitude when he sent her off to call the fire department, she decided it was his turn to be put on the spot. Smiling demurely, she murmured, "That should give you plenty of time to start your fire."

He glowered at her. She thought she heard him say something about wet wood and the Boy Scouts. But when Cathlyn crossed the threadbare maroon living-room carpet, the logs in the fireplace were blazing. Teenaged girls were sprawled on the floor and draped across the lumpy, overstuffed chairs and the ancient green velvet sofa with its missing cushion. One girl was busy with a knitting project, but most just flopped and talked.

Cathlyn settled herself Indian-style in front of the orange flames and picked out the opening strains of "Camptown Races." In rollicking harmony, the girls joined in. They began to move, swaying to the rhythm of the music, and slowly, almost unconsciously, they gravitated closer and closer to Cathlyn until they formed a tight circle in front of the fire.

Marc moved inconspicuously back from the group and sat on the floor, watching and listening. He studied Cathlyn as she sang in front of the glowing fire, watching the light from the flames dance in her hair. Her face was open and relaxed, her smile spontaneous as she shared the joy of her music. A strange backdrop for such exquisite beauty, he thought to himself. And it was equally odd that he should be here enjoying it.

Cathlyn was not like any woman he'd ever known. Most of his life had been spent trying to avoid the "suitable" women his mother kept trying to hook him up with. Instead, he had chosen a string of long-legged blondes who were willing to play just for the fun of it. Whenever one got too interested in corralling him or his money, he simply moved on to the next. But Cathlyn didn't fit in either category—or in any category at all. She certainly wasn't after his money, because she didn't know he had any. She didn't act the way he'd have thought a psychologist would. She was spontaneous and unpredictable, which was what got them into situations like today. But he could not help admiring her genuine concern and affection for these girls.

He listened to the clear, young voices blend in the spontaneous harmony of "Greensleeves" and then heard Cathlyn bridge gracefully into the familiar strains of "Good Night Ladies." For the moment he was glad to be just plain Marc Harrison. From the questions she'd asked, she was obviously curious about him, and he felt slightly guilty about misleading her. But it was only temporary. For once he wanted to develop a relationship that wasn't complicated by power, money, and the Harrison name.

Cathlyn set her guitar aside and said quietly, "Sorry, but that's all we have time for tonight. Tomorrow is a school day."

Amid gripes and grumbles, the girls moved in the general direction of the stairs leading up to the bedrooms, with Jean right behind them, obviously ready to hurry the bedtime operation along.

As the room cleared out, Marc joined Cathlyn in front of the fire.

"I'm really impressed by the girls, and by your rapport with them," he told her as he sat down with his legs stretched out alongside her. "Most of them have probably had a pretty rough go of it, and they don't have much of a future."

Cathlyn smiled to herself before she answered. "That's not necessarily true," she said, looking into his eyes. "Some of them may end up with Ph.D.s." She could see his skepticism.

"Isn't that a bit optimistic?" he countered. It was exactly the response she'd expected. She could have given him a flippant reply, but suddenly that wasn't enough. He was sitting very close to her, and Cathlyn felt totally comfortable with him. She remembered what he had said earlier. It was as if they had known each other for a very long time. For some reason she couldn't fully understand, she wanted to tell him more.

"I suppose it is optimistic," she said quietly. "But it's certainly possible. I've got a Ph.D., and I was one of these kids once."

He stared at her, not quite comprehending. "You?" He tried to picture her as a young, homeless girl, struggling on her own. It didn't fit. She was poised and lovely. Even in jeans and an old T-shirt, Cathlyn had the quiet assurance that didn't come from growing up in a halfway house. He reached toward her, gently touching her shoulder. "That doesn't make any sense," he said with a puzzled expression. "You're telling me this is the kind of place where you grew up?"

"It's a long story," Cathlyn told him, wondering now that she had begun whether she really wanted to continue. The memories came rushing back, and she looked away from Marc to study the patterns in the glowing embers of the fire. "I ran away from boarding school when I was sixteen, and wound up in San Francisco," she explained. "But before I got into real trouble, a priest picked me up on a street corner and took me to a place a lot like Angel House. I was one of the lucky ones."

She hesitated, and he stroked her shoulder, wanting her to go on. "And you stayed there?" he prompted.

"Only for a few months, until I got my head together."

"Why did you take off in the first place?" he questioned.

Cathlyn looked up at him. She hadn't realized how hard it was going to be to talk about her past. "At the time I'd have told you it was because nobody understood me," she answered slowly. "It was years before I knew what I really was running away from."

Still touching her shoulder, Marc shifted his position until Cathlyn rested against him. She forced herself to go on. "From the outside my family looked perfect. . . ." Cathlyn lowered her eyes. "Except it was nothing but a facade. My parents were so hung up with wealth and social position that they didn't care about anything else," she continued, a hint of bitterness in her voice. "My father was keeping a mistress. My mother pretended not to know. My sister whirled through her debut like nothing was wrong. It was as though nothing else mattered as long as we had lots of money and maintained the right image. Finally, one day, I just couldn't handle it anymore. I couldn't deal with the emptiness of our lives."

Marc took her hand in his. He sensed how painful this was for her. "Did you ever go back home?" he asked.

"Yes, for a while," she answered. "I finally realized I couldn't solve the problems by running away. And it was better once I found out I could set my own values, no matter where I lived." Finding the beginning of understanding in his eyes, she continued, "As soon as I could, I went my own way and concentrated on what I thought was important. It sounds trite, but I guess it has something to do with learning to be true to yourself."

"That's why you became a psychologist?"

"I suppose so." She nodded. "I've always thought people are more important than things."

He studied her thoughtfully. He'd inadvertently made a very good choice when he opted not to tell her who he was. She'd see his life-style as a symbol of the very thing that had hurt her so badly. Maybe, when she knew him better, she'd understand his own rebellion, which had followed a different course from hers. But first she had to accept him, apart from everything else, and that would take time.

Marc squeezed her hand. "I'm beginning to see why helping with Angel House means so much to you."

Cathlyn's face relaxed in a semblance of a smile. "It's one of the ways I can repay some of the people who helped me," she told him. "Angel House really is important, Marc. It can give these kids a future."

"I hadn't thought about it like that," Marc admitted. He stared at the dying fire, still cradling Cathlyn's hand in his. The contact he'd had with Angel House suddenly seemed empty. In spite of all the money he'd contributed, the only thing he'd known about it was that it was some kind of orphanage. He made a lot of different charitable donations. The primary criterion had always been his accountant's assurance that they were unshakable tax deductions. Maybe it was time to see what some of that money was actually accomplishing—and maybe even to give something more than money.

Cathlyn frowned and looked curiously at Marc. "Why have I told you all this?" she wondered aloud. "I never discuss my past."

He squeezed her hand. "Maybe because of the night and the fire," he ventured, "and because I want you to talk to me. I want to know all about you, Cathlyn, what you think and how you feel."

"But why?" she questioned.

"I don't know." His eyes held hers. "I just do." He pulled her to his feet and then put his hands lightly on her cheeks. "This is one of the strangest days I've ever spent," he told her. "Thank you, Cathlyn."

"You're welcome," she answered softly, wondering what she'd done.

Chapter Four

THE DOORBELL RANG over and over. Relentlessly. Cathlyn poked her head out from under her quilt only far enough to read the numbers on her alarm clock. Surely it wasn't Marc. It was much too early. Granted, he had been around a lot during the last few weeks. Ever since the day at Angel House, he'd called her regularly and sometimes had just shown up at her door to take her out for ice cream or go for a walk in the park. Seeing him or hearing his voice never failed to stir the now familiar thrill of anticipation.

Cathlyn opened one eye and looked at the clock again. No, it couldn't be Marc, not this early, she decided. He had specifically said he would come after lunch and she should figure out something they could do outdoors to enjoy the spring weather. But it was only eight o'clock, and it was Saturday, and they'd been out so late. . . . She slipped back into a half sleep, nestled in a cloud of happy thoughts.

Then heavy pounding punctuated the ringing of the doorbell, sending Cathlyn bolt upright. "All right, just a minute," she called out, dragging herself out of bed. She pulled on her blue quilted robe and padded barefoot toward the front door. "Who's there?" she asked, stifling a sleepy yawn.

"It's me . . . Jean," answered the impatient voice on the other side of the door. "Hurry up and let me in."

Cathlyn unhooked the chain and pulled open the door. "What are you doing here at this hour on a Saturday morning?"

"Have I got hot news for you!" Jean exclaimed. She pulled off her jacket and dropped it on top of a white lacquered chest. "Put the coffee on. I brought some Danish for breakfast."

"This had better be important," Cathlyn muttered as she followed Jean into the compact, but efficient, kitchen. Like the rest of Cathlyn's apartment, it was a bright, cheerful room with splashes of primary color vibrant against white walls.

"I guarantee it'll wake you up," Jean assured her. Pausing dramatically, she settled herself on a white caned chair at the small kitchen table. "After all this time I finally figured out Marc Harrison," she proclaimed. She began to rummage through her purse. "It was really simple if I just weren't so bad about names."

"You've lost me." Cathlyn frowned. As Jean had predicted, she was now fully awake. She was also vaguely apprehensive. Jean was acting as if she'd solved some great mystery, and Cathlyn hadn't acknowledged there was any mystery to solve. She sat down across the table from Jean while she waited for the coffee to perk, watching her friend uneasily.

After much searching, Jean pulled an envelope from the bottom of her purse. "I found this when Tom was going over some tax records the other night." She held it out to Cathlyn.

Cathlyn took the envelope and reached inside. She studied the contents with a puzzled expression on her face. Jean had given her photocopies of twelve checks for one thousand dollars each, all neatly typewritten and made out to Angel House. She was about to ask Jean what her point was when she saw the signature on the top check, blurred by the copying machine, but still readily distinguishable. Cathlyn drew in a sharp breath and flipped through the stack of papers. Every check had been signed by Marc Harrison.

"How long have these been coming?" she asked, still studying the checks.

"Every month for almost four years," Jean answered. "Except for this month. That top one you're holding is the last one with his signature. This month we got one for an identical amount, but it came from a trust fund."

"I see," Cathlyn said quietly. But she didn't see at all. If these were from Marc, why was he hiding it from her? He was apparently a major contributor to Angel House and had been for a long time. Yet he'd acted like he'd never heard of Angel House. It didn't fit. Who was Marc Harrison, anyway? Where would he get this kind of money?

Cathlyn's stomach lurched ominously. Even after all these weeks of going out with him, Cathlyn realized that in many ways, she knew less about Marc than she did about many of her casual acquaintances. He'd talked to her about everything else imaginable. But when the conversation turned to his background or his work, he always dodged her questions or deftly changed the subject. She knew he had a brother, that his mother and father were living, and that his father was a lawyer. She'd never met them; nor, come to think of it, had she ever met any of his friends or been to his office or his apartment.

"You still with me?" Jean inquired.

"I guess so," Cathlyn mumbled. She was growing more and more uneasy. "What does Tom think about all this?" she prodded.

Jean opened the white sack she'd brought and placed two pastries on napkins in front of them. "Tom said I shouldn't tell you," she admitted. "He says a lot of people contribute to Angel House on a regular basis and it doesn't mean anything, and the way Marc Harrison chooses to conduct his personal life is his own business." Jean fidgeted in her chair, then looked up at Cathlyn. "But I came, anyway, because I thought you should know."

"You were right," Cathlyn assured her, "except it doesn't seem to make much sense."

"I'm not sure about that." Jean was watching her carefully.

"I can tell you've got a theory," Cathlyn remarked dryly. "Go on." She poured them both a cup of coffee and then wrapped her fingers around the steaming mug while she braced herself for Jean's next revelation.

"Well, after I found the copies of the checks, I spent most of the day trying to put it all together. We do get regular contributions, but that's one of the biggest. Then I remembered his cashmere coat and how he paid for the pizza bash without batting an eye—"

"And the way he interrupted me that first day

you met him, before I could tell you his last name," Cathlyn cut in.

"Yes, I'd forgotten that," Jean said thoughtfully, taking a sip of her coffee.

They were silent for a moment before Cathlyn looked up at her friend. "So what does it all mean? Who *is* Marc Harrison, and what's he up to?"

"You really don't have any clues . . . after all this time?" Jean stared hard at her. "And you're the psychologist?"

"I'm beginning to wonder." Cathlyn grimaced. "I've really had my head in the sand, haven't I?"

Jean smiled sympathetically. "Let's just say you weren't working overtime. But haven't you wondered about him?"

Cathlyn took a sip of her coffee. "Frankly, yes," she affirmed. "But he obviously didn't want to talk about himself, so I backed off. He accused me of playing psychologist once. . . ."

Jean filled in the silence. "And you were scrupulously keeping your personal and professional lives separate."

"Something like that," Cathlyn agreed. "He told me he was in construction, and I took him at his word." She looked at her friend sheepishly. "I wasn't looking for any problems. I was having too much fun."

"How much does he know about you?"

Cathlyn thought back to that first night at Angel House, when they had talked in front of the fire. "A whole lot," she admitted.

"About your parents and everything?" Jean queried.

Cathlyn nodded.

Jean took another bite of her pastry, still watching Cathlyn carefully. "You really like him, don't you?"

Cathlyn hesitated, but she knew the answer. "Yes," she answered slowly, "I guess I do."

"That's what I was afraid of," Jean said, "because there's more. It's what I spent so long trying to remember. I knew there was something else about him, and it finally clicked." Jean took a bite of her Danish before she continued. "Sometimes the girls watch that zoo program on television . . . you know, what's it called?"

"Zoo Parade," Cathlyn supplied quickly.

"That's it." Jean nodded. "I happened to catch it myself while the architect for one of the new zoo buildings was being interviewed." Cathlyn stared at her, not needing the rest of her explanation but listening in fascination. "The architect was Marc Harrison, the president of Harrison Associates, Inc."

Cathlyn put her pastry back down on her napkin without taking a bite. "One of the leading architectural firms in the country," she added hoarsely. As she assimilated what Jean had just told her, a stricken look crossed her face. "No wonder he's sending thousand-dollar checks to Angel House. He could buy and sell us all."

"That's probably the great understatement of the week," Jean remarked. "He's got to be one of *the* Harrisons of our illustrious North Shore—old money, power, prestige. They're worth millions."

"Jean, that's not possible," Cathlyn protested.

She was beginning to feel betrayed. What her friend was suggesting put Marc in a whole different category. "Marc Harrison is a common name," she argued.

Jean held her ground. "Not spelled that way, it isn't."

"I don't believe it." Cathlyn shook her head.

"The Marc Harrison is a playboy who runs around with show girls and is always getting in the newspaper in connection with some society function." Jean paused before she added, "And, by the way, have you noticed Marc Harrison being mentioned in the society column recently?"

"I don't read the society column," Cathlyn replied.

"Well, I do, and it's as though he's dropped out of existence in the last several weeks. Ever since he started dating you."

"Wonderful!" Cathlyn said flatly. "And what is that supposed to mean?"

"You're smart, you figure it out," Jean said around the last bite of her second Danish. "Society editors don't write about people taking walks along the lakefront or eating tacos at Cantina Maria, or going to the movies. Especially if they don't know about it."

"I guess not," Cathlyn conceded. "But it can't be true. The Marc Harrison I know is warm and gentle and funny—"

"And wears custom-tailored suits and makes big charity donations and designs buildings all over the city." Jean laughed, but the sound rang hollow to Cathlyn. "You know," her friend said more gently, "most women would be delighted to find out that the man they're dating is a millionaire."

"I guess I'm not 'most women,'" Cathlyn retorted. "Besides, he tried to hide it from me. I can't understand that. Why would he pretend to be someone else?" She couldn't even assimilate it all, let alone believe it.

"You tell me," Jean said gently. "You know him a lot better than I do."

"Maybe not," Cathlyn noted ruefully. "So what do I do now?"

"I wish I had the answer to that one," Jean said. "I suppose you're going to have to satisfy yourself about who he really is and, if I'm right, you're going to have to figure out why he's pretending not to be."

"But how?"

"That, my friend, is a good question," Jean said, standing up. "Maybe you should start by asking him."

"Thanks a lot," Cathlyn responded dismally. "You're a treasure trove of helpful advice."

Jean patted Cathlyn on the shoulder. "I'll let myself out," she said. "Call me if you need anything, or if you just want to talk. Even psychologists need an outlet once in a while."

"Thanks," Cathlyn called after her. For a long time she stared out her kitchen window at the cloud patterns floating randomly across a brilliant blue sky, and wished her life were that simple and carefree—or even as simple as she'd thought it was before Jean arrived. She made a face as she took the last swallow of her cold coffee.

By early afternoon, Cathlyn was dressed in her aqua jumpsuit waiting for Marc to pick her up. She'd done the laundry, cleaned the kitchen, and taken care of most of her other Saturday chores. But her mind had been on Marc. She simply couldn't accept the notion that he was *the* Marc Harrison, despite what Jean had said. There had to be some mistake. At the same time, Marc was clearly not telling her everything about himself. Actually, when she thought about it, she realized he'd been purposely evasive. Why? The question haunted her.

Her first impulse was to confront him and settle it once and for all. But something held her back. She'd confronted her father once, with all her adolescent zeal, thinking she'd straighten everything out, and he'd lied. Marc wouldn't do that. He wasn't like her father. At least, she hoped he wasn't. Maybe there was another approach she could use to discover the truth. If she could figure out how to get him to voluntarily reveal his identity, that would be better. What she needed to do was get him in a situation where, if he were *the* Marc Harrison, he'd have to admit it.

Cathlyn pondered for a moment. That might not be so easy. Then she remembered what Jean had said about his firm designing a building at the zoo. That meant a sign crediting the firm should be prominently displayed. Her thoughts were clicking faster now. Actually, the plan was slightly underhanded . . . Cathlyn smiled to herself as she answered Marc's knock at the door. She was being no more devious than he'd been with her. And it was time she found out what was going on.

"Hi." Marc grinned, leaning over to give her a whisper of a kiss on her cheek. His deep hazel eyes captured her like an actual embrace.

Cathlyn covered her cheek with her fingertips as if the elusive kiss might fly away without warning. She felt a surge of guilt about what she was going to do but quickly brushed it away.

"I have a present for you," Marc announced as he stepped inside the apartment. Casually he handed Cathlyn a nosegay of fresh spring flowers. "Happy May Day," he said with a broad smile.

"They're beautiful," Cathlyn exclaimed. "Miniature daffodils, purple violets"—she examined the exquisite bouquet from all sides—"and even tiny pink rosebuds." Impulsively, she threw her arms around Marc's neck and kissed him. As he pulled her to him, she felt a delicious rush of sensation. She wanted to stay there, melted against him, but that wasn't going to solve the problem. Cathlyn hesitated. Marc was considerate in so many little ways. Had he been purposely misleading her all this time? There had to be some logical explanation for whatever was going on. And that, she reminded herself, was what she was supposed to be concentrating on that afternoon.

Cathlyn pulled away and started toward the kitchen. Her mind was made up. They would go to the zoo. "I want to put these in a vase with water before we leave," she called to him. "They smell absolutely divine."

"Not so fast," Marc protested, following her through the small, inviting living room, decorated in shades of blue and white. "I liked what we were doing." Cathlyn didn't admit to him that she had too.

He walked up behind her as she stood at the sink and, pushing aside her long hair, leaned down to nuzzle the back of her neck. "Mmm, you smell good," he murmured. He nipped her on the earlobe and slipped his arms around her, pressing his body close to hers.

"Marc . . ." Cathlyn began, squirming in his arms. Marc's broad chest was strong and warm against her back, and his breath was soft against her cheek. She felt his fisherman's knit sweater rub against her bare arms, and then his warm hands pressing just beneath her breasts. She was tempted to wrap up against him and kiss him endlessly. But that wasn't the answer, she told herself decisively. She wasn't going to find out what she needed to know that way.

"Marc!" she said firmly.

"Umm," he murmured into her silky hair. His kisses floated like clouds across her cheek.

"Marc," she repeated. It took every ounce of her control to turn and pull away from him. "It takes an hour to get to the zoo, and it's getting later and later."

"The zoo?" Marc looked startled. "Since when are we going to the zoo?" He kept one arm around her.

"You told me to pick an outdoor activity for this afternoon so we could enjoy the springtime, and I've chosen the zoo," Cathlyn announced.

She was beginning to be more and more pleased with her idea. She should have no trouble at all guiding Marc toward the new exhibits that were under construction. It would be a simple matter to point out his firm's sign, comment on the name, and get him to talk about himself.

But Marc quickly made it clear that he wasn't anxious to go to the zoo. "It's a long drive," he said, resisting. "You said so yourself. Why don't we go to the aquarium instead?"

"The aquarium?" Cathlyn was undaunted. "Stay inside on such a glorious spring day and watch a bunch of fish blowing bubbles? Oh, Marc . . ." Cathlyn's disappointment rang in her voice. I hope this works, she thought, still feeling vaguely guilty.

"What's the matter with fish? I like fish. Maybe we could go fishing," he suggested hopefully.

"Marc," Cathlyn said, looking him directly in the eye, "today is my choice, and I really want to go to the zoo."

Marc had run up against her persistence before. He knew she wasn't going to give in. Maybe the best course of action would be to go to the zoo and stay as far away as possible from the new exhibits. He looked back at her thoughtfully. He wasn't ready to discuss his background with Cathlyn, not yet. He also knew his reasons for not telling her had changed. At first he'd needed to prove to himself that she was different from all the others, not that there'd really been much question about that. But now, after what she'd told him about her own background, he wasn't at all sure she could accept him if she knew. In the greatest irony of his life, he was afraid his wealth might cost him the only woman he had ever really cared about. He had to wait until they knew each other well enough that his money and his background wouldn't get in the way.

"Well?" Cathlyn prodded.

"All right," Marc agreed with a grin. "The zoo it is."

"Finally!" Cathlyn exclaimed with a sense of victory. Her plan was working, at least so far.

An hour later Marc and Cathlyn walked hand in hand through the front gate of the zoo. "Where should we go first?" Cathlyn asked, scanning a big wooden sign with arrows and pictures of animals.

"The lions," Marc said quickly.

Cathlyn frowned at the sign, trying to get her bearings. "It looks as if the lions are over to one side of the zoo. Wouldn't it make more sense to start at the back and work forward? That way we'll be nearer the parking lot if we get tired of walking." And that way we'll be sure to cover the entire area, she added silently to herself.

"When's the last time you came to the zoo?" Marc asked in a conversational tone.

"It's been years," Cathlyn answered. "So many years that my memories are of looking up at everything."

"Then you don't remember how to get around, right?"

"Right," Cathlyn conceded.

"Then, beautiful lady, I will take you on my

extra-special, super-duper zoo tour, beginning right here, because I am an absolute expert."

I'll bet, Cathlyn thought to herself. Turning around, she spotted a concession stand. "I have an idea," she offered. "Why don't we get a map? Then we'll both know where we're going."

"Out of the question," Marc declared. "You decided where we were going to spend the afternoon, so I am going to decide how. A map would spoil your joy of discovery." He put both hands on her shoulders and propelled her down a wide asphalt path.

For a moment she wondered whether they were doing an intricate dance, with her trying to entice him in one direction while he deftly led her in another. That was silly, she decided. His reaction was perfectly normal for a man who had decided to assert himself. But it wasn't going to make her task any easier. She'd just have to watch carefully for construction and hope it wasn't in an out-of-the-way place.

"Your official zoo tour guide will now take you to see the lions," Marc asserted. He took off at a brisk clip. "We're going to follow these green paw prints that have been painted on the sidewalk," he continued in proper tour-guide fashion. "Watch out for all hazardous objects, including helium-filled balloons . . ." He ducked to avoid being hit in the face.

"Cub Scout troops . . ." He wove Cathlyn through a maze of little boys in bright blue uniforms.

"And, most of all, toddlers with sticky cotton candy." Marc came to an abrupt halt to avoid colliding with an unsteady little moppet carrying a cone of pink spun sugar nearly as big as she was. "That particular hazard is especially dangerous below the knees," he remarked.

Marc took off again, walking so fast that Cathlyn found herself panting for breath as she tried to keep pace with him. At that speed she realized she'd probably miss the construction if they tripped over it. "Hey, can't we slow down," she said with a gasp, dropping several steps behind. "We're missing all the beautiful spring scenery."

"Glad you pointed that out," Marc said, decreasing his speed only slightly. "On your left you will notice a stand of forsythia bushes alive with brilliant yellow color, and on your right you will see a bed of stately red tulips, graciously planted and nurtured by the Zoo Ladies' Garden Society. If you look carefully at the center of the tulip bed, you will be able to discern a plump robin—that favorite herald of the spring season—gathering bits of grass for her nest." Without stopping for breath, he continued. "Be sure to keep following the green paw prints, which will turn left at the next corner."

"Marc!" Cathlyn cried, coming to an abrupt halt. "I refuse to race through the zoo like we were being chased by a herd of stampeding giraffes." She folded her arms across her chest and glared up at him.

"Giraffes don't stampede," he corrected, walking back and resting his hands on her upper arms. "Besides, where's your sense of adventure?" he asked, his eyes twinkling.

"I have just as much sense of adventure as

anyone you know," she said, hotly defending herself. "I just can't walk that fast, especially in these shoes." She pointed down at her canvas espadrilles.

"You should have worn walking shoes," he observed. She glanced at his feet and saw that he was wearing sleek leather walking shoes. She'd seen an advertisment for shoes like that somewhere, but she couldn't remember where. She looked carefully at the rest of his clothes. The tan cords had an almost silky texture but without sheen. They appeared slightly worn, yet showed no sign of wrinkling or bagging at the knees as cords often did. The fisherman's knit sweater was medium weight, made of soft, fine yarn in an intricate pattern. Marc Harrison was what a fashion consultant would call impeccably dressed for the occasion. But he wore his clothes so casually, so comfortably, that they blended into his overall image. It was definitely time to find out more than she already knew about this man. Cathlyn looked over his shoulder, searching for construction equipment.

Seeing none, she took a different tack. "We will now spend a moment meditating on the beauty of the season that surrounds us," she said sweetly. "We will concentrate on those gentle signs of spring, which are so often missed when we rush through life." She pointed upward. "Notice the bright azure blue of the sky, an unblemished perfection interrupted only by an occasional fluffy white cloud. Can you feel the gentle breeze caressing your cheeks? Do you smell the rich, fertile earth?"

"I do," Marc said quietly, his hands still on her arms.

"Good," Cathlyn said with relief. "Then you are ready to resume your tour in a leisurely fashion befitting the season."

Marc's eyes, flecked with green the color of emeralds, were fixed on her. "You are unique, Cathlyn Tate," he told her.

"No more unique than you are, Marc." Cathlyn smiled up at him.

Marc's touch was as intimate as an embrace. Cathlyn's eyes met his, and the emotion that flowed between them shut out the throngs of people, the noise and the animal smells. Once again Cathlyn was deeply aware of the bond between them, so strong that it was apparent even in the midst of Saturday afternoon crowds at the zoo. She was frightened for a moment because she felt so close to this man when there might be a whole dimension of him that he had refused to share. She had to find out about Marc Harrison, quickly, before she got any more involved.

"Now we will go see the elephants," Marc said, reaching for her hand. She silently noted that he had slowed their pace considerably. But it turned out to be a small victory. By late afternoon, when the sun was dropping low in the sky, Cathlyn had not only seen the elephants, but also had zigzagged back and forth and all around the zoo many times over until she was practically dizzy. As soon as they finished making faces at the monkeys, Marc remembered it was feeding time at the lions' den—on the opposite side of the zoo. They rushed back across the main quad just in time to catch the porpoise show. After that Marc noticed a sign about feeding the tarantula.

"Boy, are we lucky," he said, beaming. "The tarantula is only fed once a month."

Naturally the insect house was miles from the porpoises. The tarantula had scarcely ingested his final bite when Marc was off and running again. It was the bears this time, twin cubs in the polar bear den, on the other side of the zoo near the south gate. Then it was the giraffes, back by the porpoises. Cathlyn kept trying to remember to look for the construction, but she was tired and her feet hurt. She attempted to draw a mental map, but their movements were so erratic that she quickly got confused. It seemed as though there was one corner of the zoo they had avoided entirely, but she couldn't be sure.

When Marc wanted to go see the tigers, Cathlyn balked. "Enough," she protested. "They're on the opposite end of the zoo, and we should have looked at them when we were in the lion's area. Marc Harrison, this is the most illogical tour I've ever taken." She didn't add that it had excluded the one thing she'd come to see but couldn't exactly ask about. Or could she?

"Aren't they building some new exhibits at the zoo somewhere?" she asked innocently.

He gave her a sharp look. "They're always building something," he said noncommittally.

Cathlyn took a deep breath. "We've seen everything else—why don't we go see that?" she suggested.

"That's clear down at the other end again," he

warned. "Besides, they're just getting under way. There's nothing to see."

He had her. She couldn't very well argue that explanation, so she tried a different approach. "How do you know so much about the zoo, anyway?" she questioned.

"I like the zoo." Marc shrugged. "It's the local answer to an African safari." He glanced at his watch and a broad grin spread across his face. "We've only got forty minutes till closing time. We can stop at the petting farm on the way out. It's right down the walk."

Whistling a jaunty tune, Marc set out again. Cathlyn sighed, wondering how her plan could have failed so miserably when there hadn't been anything standing in the way. Or had there? she wondered once more. Could it be that Marc had intentionally avoided the construction area, knowing just as she did that his name would be in full view? Again she dismissed the possibility. How could she expect anyone to include a construction site in a tour of the zoo?

Marc opened the gate to the petting farm and guided Cathlyn in ahead of him. "Oh, Marc, look—baby bunnies!" she exclaimed, her problems temporarily forgotten. She scooped up two of the soft little creatures, rubbing her cheek against their fur.

Smiling, Marc watched her for a moment and then sat down next to her on the grass. They petted a small, bleating lamb that wobbled awkwardly up to them, and then they wandered over to a glass-enclosed incubator, watching in fascination while a chick finished pecking its way out of an egg.

"This is much more fun than when I was a little girl," Cathlyn said enthusiastically. "I don't think I appreciated—or even understood—the miracle of new life until I was grown up." She crouched down and wiggled her finger through the wire fencing that enclosed a huge turkey with a bright red wattle.

"Be careful," Marc warned. "That fellow doesn't look too friendly."

"Oh, Marc, they wouldn't put something dangerous in a petting farm. Little children could get hurt." She wiggled her finger again. "See, he wouldn't hurt me." The turkey's eyes glittered menacingly.

Looking up, Marc saw the warning sign. "Watch out," he yelled, grabbing her arm. But it was a split second too late. The squawking turkey dived at Cathlyn's finger. Flapping his wings like a caricature of a giant prehistoric bird, he captured the finger in his beak.

The turkey held on tenaciously. "He won't let go," Cathlyn screamed. "Marc, do something."

"Shoo, turkey," shouted Marc, banging on the fence. "Guard, guard," he yelled. "There's someone being attacked by a turkey."

Drawn by the commotion, a crowd began to gather. "Hit the turkey with a stick," someone yelled from the rear.

"Throw rocks at him," another voice shouted.

"Oh—ouch—help!" Cathlyn screamed again as the turkey clamped down harder on her finger.

"Stop! Don't hurt that bird," called out a young

zoo attendant as he leapt over the fence into the turkey's enclosure. "He's a rare specimen."

"Just make him let go of my finger," Cathlyn pleaded. Tears welled up in her eyes as the turkey shook his head back and forth with her finger still locked in his beak.

"Here, George . . . here, gobble, gobble, gobble," the attendant called, offering an enticing handful of corn. "Come on, big fellow."

The turkey cocked his head to one side and listened. The crowd grew silent. "Come on, George . . . gobble, gobble," the attendant coaxed again. With one last shake the turkey finally let loose of Cathlyn's finger and waddled toward his keeper.

The crowd burst into applause, and Marc put his arm around Cathlyn, helping her stand up. Her finger dripped with blood.

"You have to take the lady to the first-aid station to sign a release form and let the doctor check out her finger," the attendant directed. "Insurance regulations."

"I don't want to go." Cathlyn was both angry and embarrassed, and all she wanted to do was go home.

"We don't have much choice," Marc answered sympathetically. "Your finger is bleeding a lot." He gave Cathlyn a quick, reassuring squeeze and led her through the crowd toward the office. She protectively held the bleeding finger behind her. What a dumb thing to have happen, she thought irritably. It was bad enough to get bitten, but by a turkey? She squeezed the finger tighter. It hurt a whole lot.

A bearded man in sandals met them at the door of the first-aid station. "You must be the lady who was bitten by the turkey," he said. "They just called about you."

Cathlyn nodded miserably.

"I'm Dr. Stein." He extended his hand in a friendly gesture.

"I can't shake. It's my right hand." Cathlyn sniffed. Marc shook the doctor's hand instead.

"Come on in," Dr. Stein directed, holding the door for them. "Let me have a look at that finger."

The first-aid station was a single room, cluttered but clean, with a bookcase, a cabinet filled with medical supplies, and a large metal desk mounded with papers. Cathlyn sat in a wooden chair, her hand resting on a table which was covered with clean towels, while the doctor gently cleaned and examined her finger. Marc stood behind her, his hands lightly kneading her shoulders.

"You've got some nasty lacerations," the doctor observed, pressing hard above the wound to stop the dripping blood, "but I don't think you'll need stitches. A couple of steri-strips should do the job, but your finger will be sore for quite a while."

Cathlyn winced, and Marc patted her sympathetically.

The doctor finished cleaning the wound, applied the butterfly bandages, and then wrapped the finger with gauze and tape until it stuck out from Cathlyn's hand like a fat, white banana.

"When was your last tetanus shot?" the doctor inquired.

"I don't know," Cathlyn answered innocently.

The doctor swabbed her upper arm, and before she could protest, Cathlyn had been stuck with a needle. "That adds insult to injury," she complained as she signed the release forms awkwardly with her left hand.

"Take her home and put her to bed," the doctor directed Marc. He gave Cathlyn a handful of gauze squares. "Change the dressing daily and call your family doctor if you notice any redness or swelling." He grinned. "Be sure to tell him you were bitten by a turkey."

Cathlyn didn't answer. She and Marc left the office and started toward the car. It was past closing time, and the zoo was nearly empty. When they passed the turkey's enclosure, Marc stopped, took her in his arms, and kissed her.

"As I told you when we first came into the zoo," he said, "you are definitely unique."

"Thanks a lot," Cathlyn replied, looking at her throbbing finger. "I'm no doubt the first date you've ever had who's been bitten by a turkey." Marc hugged her tighter, and she could feel him stifling his laughter.

Chapter Five

❖❖❖

EARLY MONDAY MORNING, Cathlyn crept silently into her office. If she were stationed at her desk behind a mountain of work when her secretary arrived, she could circumvent a whole lot of questions about her finger.

"Good morning, Dr. Tate," a cheerful voice greeted her from behind the reception desk. Quickly Cathlyn hid her hand behind her back.

"You're here early," she commented to Shirley, skirting the desk as inconspicuously as possible and moving toward the door to her inner office.

"I wanted to catch up on these insurance forms," Shirley explained, leaning out through the opening in the glass panel and resting her chin in her hands. "I can't seem to get to them with all the people and the phone calls. You know, Dr. Tate, you really are working too hard."

"Yes, I know, Shirley," Cathlyn agreed. She'd heard the lecture in its entirety several times already. Somewhat awkwardly she eased sideways into her office, keeping her hand behind her. After struggling out of her coat, she sank back into her desk chair, kicked off her shoes, and propped her feet on another chair.

"I hurt everywhere," she sputtered to herself. "My feet hurt from walking a million miles at the zoo, my finger hurts from being bitten by that damn turkey, and my head hurts because my feet and my finger hurt. And I don't know one thing more about Marc Harrison than I did before."

"Are you talking to me?" Shirley appeared in the doorway with a steaming mug of coffee.

"Not really," Cathlyn muttered ungraciously.

"My, my," twittered Shirley, "aren't we in a testy mood this morning!" She set the coffee in front of Cathlyn. "Maybe this will help." She scrutinized Cathlyn carefully. "Unless it's on an empty stomach. I don't suppose you've had anything to eat today?"

"No"—Cathlyn frowned—"and I don't know why everyone is always making such an issue of food. Marc is always trying to get me to eat."

"I see," Shirley said smugly. "Love problems. Did you have a fight?"

"No."

"Then he proposed?" Shirley virtually quivered with excitement at the prospect.

"No, he didn't propose."

"Too bad." Shirley sighed dramatically. "Well, if your love life isn't the problem, then you must be hungry. I'll go down to the deli and get you a bagel with cream cheese."

"I don't want a bagel," Cathlyn said with a scowl.

"I'll get it toasted," Shirley declared on her way out. "You need something to sink your teeth into besides me."

"Sorry," Cathlyn called after her.

"Don't worry about it," came the answer. "Psychologists have inner hostilities too."

Cathlyn grimaced. She hated it when Shirley was patronizing. Her inner hostilities were none of anybody's business. She swallowed two aspirin and propped her arm on a stack of books, hoping her finger would stop throbbing if she elevated it. The first item on her agenda was to evaluate several printouts of research statistics. Cathlyn stared at the tidy columns of figures for several minutes but found herself totally uninspired. Maybe I'll call Jean, she thought. She glanced at her watch. It would be a good time; the girls all would have left for school.

"You what?" Jean squealed, and Cathlyn held the phone away from her ear.

"I told you, I was bitten by a turkey, probably a killer turkey."

"I don't believe it," Jean sputtered, laughing hard. "And all for nothing?"

"A total washout," Cathlyn reported. "I didn't even get a glimpse of any construction."

"Do you think he intentionally tried to avoid it?" Jean asked.

"I wondered about that, but if you were taking someone around the zoo, would you go look at a construction site?"

"You've got a point," Jean agreed. "Look, why don't you approach him calmly and directly. Ask him what's going on." Jean giggled. "If you had done that in the first place, you might never have tangled with that turkey."

"Don't rub it in," Cathlyn retorted, glowering at her bandaged finger. "I still think there's a better way."

"You don't give up, do you?" Jean remarked. Then, without waiting for a reply, she exclaimed, "Wait—I've got it! You said he was really sympathetic about your finger, right?"

"Right," Cathlyn confirmed.

"So thank him by taking him to lunch."

"But I don't see how that—" Cathlyn began.

"Think, dummy," Jean retorted impatiently. "Go to some splashy, public place where he's sure to be recognized if he's really Marc Harrison."

"Like Rive Gauche!" Cathlyn locked in on the idea. "I think you've got something," she exclaimed, the first smile of the morning spreading across her face. "I'll call you later in the week," she promised. "I've got a reservation to make."

By the time Shirley returned with the hot bagel, Cathlyn was humming a chorus of "Oh, What a Beautiful Morning" and marking off entries in the columns of figures before her. "Great," she said, taking the bagel. "I'm starving." She bit hungrily into the chewy bread.

"Talk about a personality swing," Shirley observed dryly. Then she spotted Cathlyn's bandaged finger. "What did you do to your hand?" she demanded.

"Oh, that," Cathlyn dismissed it. "A turkey bit me."

"Could I have that one more time?" Shirley stared at her.

"A turkey bit me when I was at the zoo on Saturday," Cathlyn elaborated, taking another enormous bite of her bagel. "Marc was so nice about the whole thing that I'm going to invite him to lunch at Rive Gauche. Except I don't think I'll tell him where we're going. I want it to be a surprise." She stuffed the rest of the bagel in her mouth.

"A turkey bit you, so you're taking Marc to the ritziest restaurant in town, but you're keeping it a surprise?" Shirley shook her head. "You've got more problems than I thought."

"And what is wrong with taking Marc to Rive Gauche?" Cathlyn demanded, sitting up very straight.

"Nothing, I suppose, except it costs an arm and a leg, and you don't usually hobnob with that crowd," Shirley observed bluntly.

"Variety is good for us once in a while," Cathlyn decreed as she shuffled her papers and pointedly turned her attention back to her work.

On Friday morning Cathlyn sailed into the office dressed in a raspberry-pink dress and a straw picture hat with a tulle bow.

"The breath of spring has just arrived on the twenty-seventh floor of the Hartford Building," Shirley observed.

"Why, thank you," Cathlyn replied grandly. "I'm in the mood to be noticed."

"Marc is the focus of all this, I presume?" Shirley chuckled.

"Of course," Cathlyn confirmed. "Please buzz me when he comes in."

"The very moment he arrives," her secretary promised.

When Shirley finally called her on the intercom, Cathlyn quickly ran a comb through her hair and put on her hat. Then, taking a deep breath, she glided out to the reception room.

Marc rose to his feet instantly and took her in his arms. "You look absolutely lovely," he said, kissing her on the cheek.

"Thank you." Cathlyn fluttered her long eyelashes.

"Ahem," Shirley said loudly. "I do hate to interrupt this, but your cab is waiting down at the front entrance." Shirley replaced the phone in its cradle.

"Then we'd better go," said Marc, never taking his eyes from Cathlyn. He had never seen her look so beautiful. Her cheeks were pink and her eyes looked even more breathtakingly blue. He longed to stroke the glistening hair that tumbled from beneath that funny hat, which, on her, was the ultimate accent for an exquisite picture.

"Have a good time," Shirley called as they left the office.

Once inside the cab, it was a short ride to Rive Gauche. Marc was passingly curious where they were going, but he didn't ask. Cathlyn obviously had made her plans carefully, even down to giving the cabbie advance instructions on their destination. She seemed very pleased with herself, Marc noted, looking at her with a twinge of amusement. She was so beautiful.

"Here we are," Cathlyn announced when the cab swung into the circular drive in front of Rive Gauche and pulled to a stop before the wine-colored awning. Immediately a uniformed doorman swept open the taxi door, holding it while he waited for Marc and Cathlyn to emerge.

Damn, thought Marc. He'd never expected her to do something like this. If he as much as stepped out of the cab, a dozen people would recognize him. The maître d' would call him by name and inquire about his health. Someone would certainly stop by their table, expecting an introduction. More than anywhere else in town, Rive Gauche was the place people went to see and to be seen. He knew, because he'd played the game too. Now what was he going to do?

"Marc?" Cathlyn took his hand and scooted slightly toward the door.

When there's nothing else to do, punt, he thought silently. "Cathlyn," he boomed. "How could you think of such a thing? I wouldn't dream of letting you pay for an expensive meal like this!"

Looking stricken, Cathlyn turned toward him. "But, Marc, I told you it was my treat for all your help with my hurt finger. I want to do it." She started to get out of the cab, but Marc grabbed her arm.

"We're not going in there," he announced firmly.

"Oh, yes we are," Cathlyn said, defying him.

"Are you folks getting out or not?" interrupted the cabbie.

"We are not," Marc stated emphatically. He reached across Cathlyn and slammed the taxi door shut, ducking back quickly when the startled doorman caught his eye. "Oak and Michigan," he ordered the driver.

"Marc!" Cathlyn cried out in sheer frustration. "That's not fair. I had this lunch all planned." She stiffened angrily as Marc took her in his arms.

"I can't let you splurge like that—spend all that money on one lunch," he whispered, lightly stroking her back. "I'll think of something else, something special." His lips tenderly found hers, and she felt him soften the edges of her anger.

"But, Marc—" she protested, pulling away.

"No *buts,*" he warned, still holding her.

Cathlyn closed her eyes and pressed her lips back to his. She felt her determination waning as she melted against him in a deep, gentle kiss. The world seemed right when Marc took her in his arms. She could easily let herself float away with him on a cloud of hazy fantasies. Nothing else seemed very important.

Marc released her slowly and leaned back in the seat, looking out over the sparkling blue waters of Lake Michigan. "I've got an idea," he said, snapping his fingers. "Let's have a picnic along the lakefront. We'll pick up a bottle of Chablis, some Brie, and a loaf of French bread."

"A picnic? Today?" Cathlyn blinked.

"Stop at the next corner," he directed the driver, and then turned enthusiastically to Cathlyn. "There's a gourmet food shop down the street. They should have everything we need."

"But, Marc, we're not dressed for a picnic," Cathlyn observed hesitantly.

"Do you care?"

The way he looked at her, there was only one answer. "No," she said, "not at all."

"Then where's that sense of adventure you're always talking about?"

"The last time I followed my sense of adventure, a turkey bit me," Cathlyn said soberly, holding up her bandaged finger.

Marc kissed her finger lightly. "There are no turkeys on the beach," he promised, helping her from the cab and directing the driver to wait for them.

"And if a sea gull flies overhead at a strategic moment?" she inquired as they entered the gourmet shop.

"Keep your hat on," he answered drolly.

By the time Marc and Cathlyn arrived at the beach, nothing sounded better than a picnic on the sand. They toasted the springtime with white wine in clear plastic glasses, and both smiled contentedly as they finished the last bits of some French pastries Marc had discovered in the rear of the gourmet shop. The light lake breeze had lost its chill, and the water, so rough and angry a few weeks before, lapped gently at the shore. Cathlyn removed her hat, along with her high-heeled pumps, and laid them beside her on the sand. Marc tossed his suit coat next to the shoes and rolled up his sleeves. They both leaned back, letting the hot rays of the early-afternoon sun soak their winter-white skin.

"Talk about a beautiful day," Marc said lazily, resting his head in Cathlyn's lap.

"It's perfect," she agreed. With her fingers she brushed several stray wisps of hair back from his forehead.

"No regrets about the restaurant?" Marc asked after a moment.

Cathlyn hesitated, remembering that she'd been railroaded and should be angry. But as the breeze rippled her skirt and a lone sea gull called out from far down the beach, she felt a world apart from the city that towered at her back. How could she possibly have regrets when she was so deliriously happy here with him in the gentle sunshine? When he looked up at her, her eyes were smiling. "No regrets, Marc," she told him. "Absolutely no regrets."

Marc lay silently for a moment, toying with the idea of telling Cathlyn the whole truth. The charade had seemed perfectly reasonable at first. He hadn't considered it a deception. But then he'd begun to care about her, and that changed everything. The longer it went on, the more uneasy he got. Now might be a good time to tell her. They were relaxed and happy together, with the breeze from the lake soothing them. He opened one eye and squinted up at Cathlyn. The wind tossed her hair lightly over her shoulders. Her nose was already sunburned.

"You're very beautiful, Cathlyn," he began.

"Thank you," she answered softly.

He sat up and looked directly at her. "I need to tell you something." Her vivid blue eyes were so gentle and so trusting. My God, he thought. What if he told her now and she wasn't ready? She had to care about him enough that it didn't matter who he was. And enough to forgive him for not telling her before. Otherwise he might lose her before they'd even had a chance.

"What is it, Marc?" she pressed gently.

He hesitated for a split second, torn by the inner debate. "I want to go run in the waves," he said abruptly. He couldn't tell her. Not yet. He pulled Cathlyn to her feet.

"Run in the waves?" Cathlyn made no attempt to hide either her surprise or her disappointment. She didn't know what it was he'd started to say to her. She could only suspect. But whatever door Marc Harrison had started to open had been slammed shut again, and she knew instinctively that any efforts she made to change that would be futile.

"Come on," he urged, pulling on her hand.

"I have stockings on," she protested.

"Take them off," Marc directed. "Don't waste a beautiful day."

Impulsively Cathlyn reached up under her skirt and wiggled out of her panty hose, while Marc took off his shoes and socks and rolled up his pant legs.

"Let's go," she cried, grabbing his hand. With the abandon of children, they raced across the sun-warmed sand directly into the icy water of the lake.

"It's freezing," Cathlyn screamed as a spray of water stung her legs.

"Keep running with me," Marc yelled back, holding fast to her hand. They darted along the water's edge, jumping over piles of frothy, white foam and skirting swirls of seaweed. They ran the length of the beach before they stopped, laughing and panting with exhilaration. Marc reached for her and she fell, shivering, into his arms.

"Up there," he said, pointing to a large pile of boulders a way back from the beach. "If we climb up on the rocks, the sun will warm us up."

Shaking from the cold, and breathing hard from the exertion, Cathlyn followed him to a flat rock near the top. He flopped down, and she snuggled close to him.

"You're really cold, aren't you?" he asked, slipping his arms around her.

"I'll be all right in a minute," she said, shivering.

Marc leaned down and kissed her, a brief, gentle kiss. "Your lips feel like ice," he said, pulling back slightly and scrutinizing her carefully. "And they're turning blue," he added. He ran his finger along the edge of her lower lip.

"But they won't stay that way," Cathlyn predicted. She wrapped her arms around his neck and kissed him back, a long, sensuous kiss that obliterated the sensation of cold even before warming her body. She burrowed happily against him and let her head rest in the protective hollow of his shoulder. They sat lost in each other, encircled by the lake breeze, lulled by the soft slapping of the waves.

"Happy?" he asked her.

"So very happy," she murmured. It was an unnecessary question. With a deep sigh of contentment she feathered a path of light kisses down the side of Marc's neck, darting the tip of her tongue playfully at the drops of water in the hollow of his throat.

Marc drew in a sharp breath and pulled her tightly to him. His hands, where they gripped her shoulders, were hotter than the sun. "You're not shivering anymore," he whispered. His lips found the sensitive spot behind her earlobe.

"How could I be?" she murmured, stroking the back of his neck. She ran her fingers along the inside of his collar until she reached the short, dark curls of hair at the open neck of his shirt. "Why is it you make me feel like this?" she asked softly, waves of pleasure surging through her.

"Like what?" he questioned. His tongue teased her earlobe, before tracing a tingling path across her cheek. His lips, as full and warm as her own, found her mouth.

As she moved against him, her heartbeat quickened. "You know very well like what," she answered when his lips left hers.

"Yes, Cathlyn," he told her, his voice hoarse. "I do know. Every time we're together, I feel it more and more."

"So do I, Marc," she told him softly. They sat quietly for a long time, each lost in thought, until the warmth of the gentle sunshine began to fade.

Reluctantly Marc stood up and helped Cathlyn climb down the rocks. Together they walked slowly and silently back along the beach. The spontaneous happiness that had sprung from the zany day together was clouded by what lay unspoken between them. But neither of them seemed to be able to talk about it. Still barefoot, they crossed the grass parkway, and Marc hailed a cab.

Chapter Six

THE NEWSPAPER WAS lying unfolded on her desk the next morning when Cathlyn breezed into her office. A short item was circled in red marker.

Frowning, Cathlyn sat down. Shirley never meddled with her morning paper. Her eyes traveled down the gossip column to the small, neat block of type within the red lines.

"Question of the day: Who was the mystery lady Marc Harrison brought to the doorstep of Rive Gauche yesterday before racing off with her in a taxi? Could she be the reason he's virtually dropped out of sight recently?"

A chill gripped Cathlyn. Her plan had worked, but not the way it was supposed to. She stared at the words again, until they blurred into one another. It really was true. Not that she'd actually doubted it, not deep inside. But now she knew for sure. There could be no more pretending. The man she thought she'd come to know so well was someone else entirely. Marc Harrison, regular guy, was, in reality, Marc Harrison, rich playboy.

And she never had succeeded in getting him to admit it. No wonder he'd refused to go to Rive Gauche. And all those excuses she'd made to herself about the day at the zoo. Missing that construction site had been no accident—he'd kept her away from it on purpose. But why? Cathlyn asked herself. Why did he do it?

Cathlyn stuffed the newspaper firmly into the wastebasket and stalked across her office to the window. She stared at the lines of cars creeping along, far below her, as the morning rush hour reached its peak. Speculating with Jean had been one thing. Seeing it all laid out in black and white was something else. Had he done it just for the hell of it? she wondered. Or had he devised some elaborate test to see how long he could get away with it? She shook her head. The whys didn't matter much anymore. The rich playboy-architect had had his fun, and now the game was over. How ironic, she thought, that she, the psychologist, the great believer in truth and honesty, had let herself be swallowed up by such a monstrous deception.

The more she thought about it, the more Cathlyn's stomach hurt. She walked slowly back to her desk and sank down on her swivel chair. She hadn't just let him deceive her, she'd wanted to be deceived. It had all seemed so perfect that she'd wanted it to be real. Even now she found herself searching for some reason behind what he'd done, some plausible explanation. But this was no time for excuses. She was hurt and angry, and the sooner she dealt with it, the better.

Cathlyn tapped the pencil on her desk. It wasn't quite eight o'clock. Marc rarely left for work before nine. He probably wouldn't have to work at all if he didn't want to, she thought sullenly. Cathlyn felt her hurt giving way to anger. She'd been conned, purposely and systematically conned. And she wasn't about to sit back and take it. Grabbing her coat, Cathlyn flew out her office door, barely avoiding a head-on collision with Shirley, who was carrying a sack of sweet rolls from the deli.

"Oh, Dr. Tate," Shirley said with a gasp. "Did you find the newspaper?"

"Yes, I found the newspaper." Cathlyn did not elaborate. What she was about to do was none of anyone's business. "I'm going out," she announced. "If you don't hear from me by one o'clock, cancel my meeting with the computer man. It's the only thing on the calendar."

"Dr. Tate? Are you all right?" Shirley looked worried.

"I'm just fine," Cathlyn declared with deadly calm. "I have some long-overdue business to attend to." Then she stopped, suddenly realizing she didn't even know where Marc Harrison lived. She'd asked him a couple of times, but he'd been vague, saying he had an apartment near the river. When she'd pressed him, he'd only laughed and said it defied description but that he'd take her and show it to her soon. But he never got around to it. Now she understood why. *Damn, I've been stupid,* she thought, chastising herself.

Cathlyn turned back toward her secretary. "By the way, Shirley," she began as casually as possible, "do you have Mr. Harrison's address?"

"Ah, 'Mr.,' is it?" Shirley responded tartly. "*Mr.* Harrison owns a penthouse suite in River Place. But, Dr. Tate, I really think—"

"Thank you, Shirley," Cathlyn said, cutting her off abruptly. She was out the door before her startled secretary could proclaim whatever it was she really thought.

Cathlyn stared out of the taxi at the blur of people and cars moving back and forth in front of towering buildings with endless rows of windows. Why, she asked herself over and over again, why had he hidden who he was? And why, she thought, nagging herself, had she let him? If she'd tried to talk it out with him, which was exactly the advice she'd have given anyone else in her situation, the issue would have been resolved long ago. Instead she'd ignored all the warning signs because she hadn't wanted to see them. She'd surrendered to her feelings and left herself open to be deeply hurt. Why? She refused to face the obvious answer.

Instead she purposely focused on Marc's deception. Block by block, her anger grew as she thought about what he had done. By the time the cab pulled up in front of River Place, Cathlyn was boiling mad. Marc Harrison had no right to treat her that way. When she was through with him, he'd be sorry he'd ever tangled with her. He could go back to his society friends and have a good laugh. She slammed the taxi door behind her.

The lobby of River Place was done in winter white. Gleaming brass chandeliers embedded with hundreds of tiny, twinkling lights dropped from the great domed ceiling. Cathlyn barely noticed. She squared her shoulders and glided purposefully past the security desk. Without breaking her stride, she nodded to the guard. He frowned, but he didn't stop her.

The slim heels of her pumps clicked on the gleaming tile walkway that curved through the expanse of white carpet. Assuming she'd find a bank of elevators around the corner at the rear of the lobby, Cathlyn kept walking, not allowing herself the slightest hesitation. One of the lessons she'd learned well was that people who look like they know what they're doing can bluff their way through almost anything. If she aroused any suspicions at all, Marc would be called before she was allowed to go up. She couldn't let that happen. This meeting was going to be on her terms for a change.

Cathlyn chose a single elevator apart from the others and studied the operating panel, trying to figure out which of the unnumbered buttons would be most likely to take her to the top floor. She settled on *P*, for penthouse, and silently the elevator whisked her upward. Her watch said 8:22. She pressed her lips together in a firm, straight line. This should take about five minutes. After it was over, she could either be back in the office by nine or go for a long drive in the country. She'd see how she felt.

The elevator doors opened into a vast, silent hallway, with dark oak parquet floors and a muted red Oriental runner down the center. She followed the runner for a distance, realizing that she must be in the central core of a building with twelve large penthouse suites, three on each side. She passed several identical walnut-paneled doors before she came to the one on the river side with a small nameplate that read HARRISON.

She rapped the brass knocker sharply and waited, shifting her weight from one foot to the other. The door opened a wide crack, just far enough for Cathlyn to see that the man on the other side wasn't Marc.

"Yes?" the male voice demanded.

Cathlyn summoned the most commanding tone she could muster. "I'm here to see Marc Harrison," she announced. She'd come this far; she might as well go on, however it turned out.

"And who may I say is calling?" inquired the voice with a British accent.

"Cathlyn Tate," she responded coldly.

"One moment, madam," the voice answered with no hint of emotion.

Cathlyn fidgeted for several seconds before she heard a chain disengage, and the door opened wide. The source of the voice turned out to be a man in a dark suit, probably in his early sixties, with a neatly trimmed beard and a very bald head. "Mr. Harrison said that I should show you to the library and he'd be with you directly," the man explained, closing the door behind Cathlyn.

"Who are you?" Cathlyn asked bluntly.

The man looked surprised. "My name is Jones," he informed her. "I assist Mr. Harrison. Please follow me."

Cathlyn refused coffee, and Jones left her alone. Looking around the room, lined floor to ceiling on two sides with books, she saw ample evidence of Marc Harrison, architect. Even her untrained eye recognized the simplicity of line and color that turned the room into a backdrop for the wall of glass that looked out across the city. From where she stood, Chicago stretched endlessly to the south, towers of glass and steel against a backdrop of blue. To the east, the sun danced across whitecapped waves, which rose up to meet the rim of the sky. It was a scene of endless power and beauty, an ever-changing panorama viewed from above.

So this was the city from Marc's perspective, she thought, leaning her forehead lightly against the window as she stared down at the tiny figures scurrying back and forth on the street. The view from the top, she laughed bitterly to herself, looking away.

"Cathlyn?" The voice in the doorway startled her, and she tensed. "What are you doing here?"

Slowly she turned to face him. His shirt was open, his hair still damp from the shower. Powerful emotions surged through her, snarling her thoughts and dulling her reflexes. She fought against the memories of his arms around her, the sweet warmth of his lips, the laughter welling in the depths of his amber eyes. Tiny shards of feeling bombarded her and then she remembered, slowly and painfully, the reasons she had come. This was the real Marc Harrison standing before her, whatever else he had led her to believe.

"What am I doing here?" she repeated coldly. "Maybe I should ask you the same thing."

"I live here," he answered.

"So I see."

He stared at her, waiting. Cathlyn's anger at him, and at herself for what she had to do, churned inside, and she turned back toward the window, staring out across the city while she searched for the right words. Suddenly he was behind her, his hands on her shoulders. "I should have told you long ago," he said softly. "How did you find out?"

"I assume you haven't read the paper," she said in a controlled voice.

"Part of it," he answered.

"The society page?"

"What did it say?" he demanded, steel in his voice.

"It seems we—or rather you—were recognized at Rive Gauche yesterday," she answered.

"Damn," he muttered under his breath. He gently kneaded her shoulders with his fingers. "That isn't the way I intended for you to find out, Cathlyn."

"Oh, it isn't?" she snapped back, wrenching from his grasp.

"No, it isn't," he replied evenly.

"If you didn't want me to read it in the newspaper, then just how did you plan that I find out? Were you going to send me an engraved announcement one day when you got around to it? Or maybe you thought you wouldn't bother to mention it at all. You were having such a good time with your little game, you figured you'd just go on playing until it bored you. Then you could walk away from it and look for another diversion."

"Cut it out, Cathlyn," he ordered, his voice so harsh that she took a step backward. His whole body was rigid. "You've got a right to be mad as hell, but that's no reason to barge in here and rant at me!"

"Then maybe you should throw me out." Cathlyn's eyes were as icy as her voice.

"I don't want to throw you out. I just want you to sit down and listen to me for a minute."

"So you can make excuses? So you can tell me your lies and deceptions were just a little oversight?" she fired back.

"I never lied to you," he asserted coldly.

"Exactly what would you call it?" she challenged.

He shoved his hands in his pockets and paced across the room. "I simply didn't tell you who I was. At first it was intentional. Later it was . . ." He hesitated. "Later it was something I couldn't seem to get myself out of."

"And that's supposed to explain everything?" she demanded.

"If you'll quit being so unreasonable, I will explain." His voice rose until he was almost shouting. "Dammit, Cathlyn, sit down."

Overwhelmed by his intensity, she sat stiffly on the very edge of a navy blue sofa facing the window. Marc planted himself directly in front of her, his arms folded across his chest. "Now, to begin with, I did not lie—" he began.

"You already said that," she interjected.

"Be quiet and listen," he ordered. "I never intended for things to get to this point. It just sort of happened."

Cathlyn glared at him, but she didn't interrupt.

"That day we met in the taxi, I knew you were something special. I couldn't get you out of my mind afterward. You were so open and so much fun. That first day I just didn't get around to telling you much about me. After that, it was on purpose. I've had some bad experiences with women, Cathlyn. Women who like money and power—"

Cathlyn's eyes narrowed, and her whole face skewed into an expression of profound disbelief. "You thought I was after your *money*?"

"I didn't think anything," Marc replied. "I didn't know you. But I did know I liked the relationship just the way it was. So I decided to keep it that way for a little while."

"Wonderful," Cathlyn retorted sarcastically. "And exactly what is your definition of a little while? Two months? Two years?"

Marc paced over to the window, and Cathlyn studied his profile against the brilliant morning sun. His body was quiet, his face pensive, as he stared out across the city. Whatever he'd done was obviously more than a game. He'd apparently had what he considered a good reason. But that didn't change the fact that he'd intentionally misled her.

"I never expected it to go on this long," Marc answered slowly. "But after the night we talked at Angel House and you told me about your family and about how you grew up, I knew my background was going to get in the way. I decided to wait until we knew each other better to tell you." He turned around and studied her intently. "And frankly, Cathlyn," he observed, "I probably made the right decision."

"I'm glad you're pleased with it," she retorted. "If you didn't have enough respect for me to be honest, then there's no point in continuing this discussion." Gathering up her purse, Cathlyn stood up.

"Wait just a minute," Marc commanded, taking a step toward her. "First you're going to answer a question. When I called you initially, would you even have gone out with me if you'd known who I was?"

"That has nothing to do with it," Cathlyn snapped.

Marc's eyes were hard. "It most certainly does," he declared. "Answer the question."

Cathlyn lowered her eyes. "Probably not," she admitted. "But there's no way you could have known that at the beginning. And after all this time you still didn't tell me."

"I almost did yesterday when we were on the beach," Marc said.

Cathlyn was silent, remembering the awkward moment. So that was what he had been about to say. "What stopped you?" she implored.

"I don't know." Marc shoved his hands in his pockets and turned away. "I guess I was afraid to tell you. I didn't want to lose you."

Cathlyn sat down and clasped her hands in her lap. She didn't know what to do. She'd come to end this relationship, to make a sharp, clean break. But now she didn't want to end it, and yet she didn't see how it could continue.

When Marc sat down beside her, Cathlyn stiffened and moved away. If she couldn't trust him before, how could she let herself trust him now?

"There's a hell of a lot you don't understand," Marc said softly.

"So why don't you enlighten me?" Cathlyn felt herself working hard to maintain a barrier between them.

"All my life people have slapped me with an image I was supposed to fit right into." Marc's voice was bitter. "From the time I was a little boy, I've heard 'You're a Harrison.' Well, I got damn sick of being a Harrison."

"You don't seem to mind some of the advantages that go along with it," Cathlyn observed, looking around.

Marc scowled at her. "I didn't go the sackcloth-and-ashes route, if that's what you mean. And I didn't let my hair grow and drop out of school and wander the streets barefoot like you did, either."

"Of course not. You went right along and did what proper Harrisons do, except you complained about it."

"Tell my father that." He laughed bitterly. "Proper Harrisons go to Harvard and become lawyers. He practically disowned me when I refused. I paid a good part of my own way through college—I'd been there three years before he even acknowledged what I was doing." Marc's voice was edged with steel. "I studied architecture because that's what I wanted. It was something I cared about, one way I believed I could make a contribution. And it was one place where I had a chance of making it on my own without riding my father's coattails." Marc began pacing again, and Cathlyn sat quietly, almost afraid to interrupt him.

"There's something else that maybe you do understand in a way," he continued bitterly. "Money and power sound really great, but there's another side to it." He stopped pacing and sat beside her again, not touching her, his eyes blazing with emotion as he spoke. "You know how money and power can screw up relationships, Cathlyn. You're never sure whether people care about you or what you can do for them. All I wanted was for once to have a normal relationship with somebody. I wanted to go to the movies and walk along the lake and eat hot dogs for dinner without anything getting in the way."

"But, Marc, that was a long time ago. I still don't understand why you kept stringing me along. Don't you trust me?"

"Dammit, Cathlyn," he exploded. "Of course I trust you."

"You have a funny way of showing it."

"What the hell was I supposed to do? Show up one night and say, 'By the way, there's something I haven't mentioned. . . .' "

"It would have been better than nothing," she shot back. "You never should have gotten yourself in that position in the first place."

"I didn't mean to," he protested. "How the hell was I supposed to know it was going to matter so much what you thought?"

"So you went ahead with this hoax because—"

"Dammit, Cathlyn, because I love you."

Cathlyn stared at him, letting his words sink in. Was he telling her that this whole wretched deception was because he loved her? She searched his face. That was exactly what he was saying. Slowly she understood something else, something she should have known all along.

She reached across the void that separated them and touched his hand. No wonder she had gone along with the hoax, wanting so desperately to believe him. She hadn't been willing to face the truth because she was falling in love with him.

"Can't you see what's happened between us?" Marc said with urgency in his voice.

"I'm only beginning to," she told him.

"And do you believe I love you?" he demanded.

Cathlyn couldn't answer him. With all of her being she wanted to trust him, and yet he had deceived her. She couldn't escape that.

His fingers gripped her arm. "Cathlyn, you've got to believe me." His voice was raw with emotion. "How can I make you understand how much I love you?"

Roughly he took her in his arms. She felt every muscle tense in the inner struggle that raged within her. Then Marc's mouth found hers in a blaze of passion that engulfed them both. He kissed her again and again, his lips possessing her and still demanding more. She dug her fingers into his back, holding on to him as though she might be swept away on the tide of emotion that swirled around them.

"Marc, I do love you," she whispered, clutching him tighter. She fell back against the sofa cushions with his body against hers, his chest pressing on her swelling breasts.

"You mean everything to me," he said

hoarsely, trailing fiery kisses across her cheek to the hollow of her throat. His lips caressed her silken skin until she cried out in ecstasy, arching her head back, her hair trailing loosely across the cushions. He twined his fingers in her curls, gripping her tightly as he raised her head until her mouth was on his. Hungrily he sought her, rimming her lips with his tongue until they were wet and slippery.

His touch fueled raging fires within her. He reached inside her suit jacket, sliding his hands along the delicate fabric of her blouse until he molded the soft curves of her breasts. Again he kissed her, his mouth moving as his hands caressed her in a building, flowing rhythm. "I want you, Cathlyn," he told her in a voice thick with desire. "I want to make love to you."

Her body screaming for him, she wound her arms around his neck. "Just keep holding me, Marc," she managed to reply. "Just don't let go."

"I won't let you go, my love," he answered tenderly. "Not now, not ever." He raised her up with one arm, deftly stripping away her clothes until she was naked to the waist. Stopping to touch her, he caressed her with his hands and then with his mouth. "My God, you're beautiful, Cathlyn," he murmured. She saw the raw desire that threatened to consume her reflected in his eyes.

His lips possessed her once again before he removed her remaining clothing and stood up to shed his own. Lying deep in the big, soft cushions, she watched him as he tossed away his shirt and pants. His body emerged, strong and powerful. She held out her hands toward him. "Marc," she cried, reaching upward.

"My God," he murmured, and he was in her waiting arms. All the wild emotion within Cathlyn poured out as she went to him, crying out his name again and again in unbearable ecstasy until, at the final moment, a piercing scream tore at her throat.

Afterward she lay against him, all her senses numbed by the consuming passion. Exhausted but complete, she looked up to find Marc's eyes glowing as he studied her face. "I've been looking for you all my life, Cathlyn," he told her softly. "Now that I've found you, I'll never let you go."

"I have no desire to go anywhere," she murmured, snuggling her head into the curve of his arm. She had given herself completely to him, and at that moment she had no need to analyze why. All she wanted was to be a part of this man she loved so much.

Cathlyn's breathing was slow and steady as she hovered on the edge of sleep, resisting because it felt so good to lie there nestled in his arms. Silently they drifted away together, as though any sound might shatter the perfect union they had shared. The last thing she remembered was Marc's soft breath against her neck before she fell asleep.

She awoke to find Marc propped on one elbow, watching her. As her eyes fluttered open, he gently brushed away a stray lock of her hair with his fingertips. She smiled up at him. "Have we been here a long time?" she asked.

"Yes, it's the middle of the afternoon," he told her. "I hope you weren't supposed to be somewhere."

She tried to remember. Everything else seemed so remote. "I don't think so. I don't want to go, anyway," she added softly.

He stroked her with gentle hands, letting his eyes sweep the length of her nude body in a lazy caress. "Neither do I," he said with a sigh. "But I think I'm getting hungry. What about you?"

Cathlyn considered that for a moment. "I think I'm absolutely starving," she said, surprised that she was.

"All that activity." He grinned. "Jones is off for the weekend, but he always leaves food when he goes on one of his jaunts." He stood up and pulled her to her feet.

"We're going to have lunch like this?" Cathlyn asked. She suddenly felt very naked.

"We could," he teased. "But if you like, I'll get you a robe."

"I like." She laughed.

Wrapped in Marc's soft velour robe, which was about three shades bluer than her eyes, Cathlyn sat in the kitchen munching crackers and cheddar cheese while Marc, wearing a dark brown robe that fell open across his chest, concocted a mushroom-and-bacon omelet. From her vantage point at the round cherry-wood table, Cathlyn could see the entire apartment, which was arranged in tiers with the kitchen at the top.

She studied the eclectic blend of new and old that flowed together in a kind of comfortable anti-style. Marc obviously liked blue and deep red, and the mellow hue of antique woods polished to a deep luster. "This is beautiful," she said in admiration.

"You are beautiful," he answered, brushing her cheek with a kiss on his way to the refrigerator.

"Did you put all this together—your apartment, I mean?" she asked.

"I did," he replied, with no hint of modesty. "I gathered together lots of things I liked, and presto!" He gave an egg a sharp crack against the edge of the bowl.

"Marc," Cathlyn began thoughtfully, "I'm still having trouble with . . . with all of this. After you think you know someone pretty well, it's hard to find out you don't know him at all."

"Cathlyn, that's not true," he argued, shaking the omelet pan. "Am I any different because I'm an architect? Or because my family has money?"

"That's not the point."

"It's exactly the point. If you'd known from the beginning, it might have gotten in the way—we might never have really known each other. I admit I should have told you, and believe it or not, I tried. But I was afraid you'd be so angry, we'd never have a chance."

"I might have been," Cathlyn acknowledged. "Actually, I was. When I came today, it was to tell you that you were despicable and I never wanted to see you again. I never intended . . ."

He set the steaming omelet, still in the pan, on a trivet in the center of the table and brought two white china plates. "But aren't you glad it worked out this way instead?"

"I guess so," Cathlyn said slowly.

"You guess so?" He turned to stare at her. "We share what was probably the most glorious moment two people could experience together, and you say 'I guess so'?"

"I didn't mean it that way, Marc," she added hurriedly. "It all just takes some getting used to."

"Then we'll spend today and tomorrow and however much longer it takes getting used to it," he declared, setting half of the omelet in front of her. "Meanwhile you get the orange juice and I'll pour the coffee."

Cathlyn was quiet while they ate. She stared out the floor-to-ceiling windows that ran across the entire side of the apartment, looking at the city below them, which stretched into endless distance. The past few hours were almost more than she could assimilate. She could never remember being so angry. Nor had she ever experienced passion so intense. Even thinking about it made her shiver inside. It was hard to believe she had wanted him so much, that she still wanted him.

But sitting there snuggled in Marc's robe, in the waning light of the afternoon, she was left to contend with cold reality. Marc was, after all, *the* Marc Harrison, and nothing could change that. He was wealthy, he was powerful, he was the symbol of everything she'd been so vehemently opposed to all her life. Once again she realized that he'd been right. If she'd known all about him from the beginning, she probably wouldn't have agreed to see him. And if she had, she would have been constantly on her guard, keeping him at a safe distance.

Although it defied logic, maybe Marc was right in another sense too. He was, after all, the same person she'd spent countless days and evenings with over the last three months. She was the only one who had changed. What he was asking of her was that she not let the Harrison power and money, and his own playboy reputation, make any difference. It was a reasonable request, except deep inside she knew it did make a difference, whether she wanted it to or not. Even if she could accept him, could she accept the life-style she'd rejected so long ago?

"Cathlyn, what's bothering you?" Marc asked gently, reaching across the table to take her hand.

"What do you mean?" she asked, returning abruptly from her reverie.

"You're very quiet. You've been thinking about everything that's happened. I can see it in your eyes."

"I just can't get used to it, I guess," she answered slowly. "Jean showed me some checks you'd sent to Angel House, and I suppose I knew then, but I didn't let myself believe it. I thought maybe if we went to the zoo and there was a sign with your firm's name near the construction, maybe we could talk about it."

"So that's what the day at the zoo was all about." Marc laughed. "I thought you'd never quit. If it hadn't been for that turkey—" He stopped short and gave her a penetrating look.

"And Rive Gauche . . . that was a setup too?" he demanded.

"Yes, I guess you could put it that way." Cathlyn lowered her eyes to her empty plate.

"So you haven't exactly been open and honest yourself," he declared flatly.

"That's not fair," Cathlyn protested. "How else was I supposed to find out?"

"You could have asked me," he suggested.

"You'd have just denied it," she retorted hotly.

"No, I wouldn't have." He let go of her hand and ran his fingers roughly through his hair. "I've tried to explain to you. I wanted to tell you. I just couldn't figure out how."

"What else haven't you told me?" she pressed.

"You assume I have a closetful of skeletons?"

"I just don't like surprises, at least not that kind of surprise." She reached across the table and clasped his hand in both of hers. "Marc," she said, "common sense tells me to be careful just in case you really are what Marc Harrison is supposed to be."

"And what is that?" he demanded coldly.

She looked directly into his eyes. "A rich playboy who uses power, toys with women, and lives only for his own enjoyment."

"That's quite an indictment." His face was sober. "Is that what you think?" He watched her carefully for a moment. "Are you afraid I'm like your father?"

The question jarred Cathlyn. Was that what she really was afraid of? Deep inside, did she think that any man with wealth and power would be unfaithful to her just as her father had been to her mother? She stared at Marc for a long time, searching his face for answers he couldn't give her. But she found love and trust that stilled her fears, and in a rush of emotion she had her answer.

"No, Marc, you're not like my father." She wrapped her fingers tightly around his. "At least not the Marc Harrison I know. He's thoughtful, compassionate, cares about people. At least that's what I believed. . . ."

"Nothing has changed, Cathlyn."

"I know that, but . . ."

"Give it some time," he urged. "What we have is too good to throw away."

"All right," she agreed slowly. "But we can't go on pretending you're someone else. You can't have one life with me and another life I'm not part of."

Marc stood up and walked around the table. Slipping his hands around her waist, he lifted her up into his arms. "From now on, Cathlyn, you'll be part of everything," he whispered into her hair. "I promise."

His words sent a chill of apprehension through Cathlyn. Could she really be happy becoming a part of all that again? Then his mouth possessed her, his lips firm and demanding, and she opened her lips to meet him. Her body molded against his, and her doubts slipped away. He kissed her once and then again, a long, deep kiss that held the promise of that hidden world the two of them had shared. Nestling her head lightly against his shoulder as his arms tightened around her, Cathlyn could see the brilliant sunset reflecting red on the whitecapped waves of the lake. She felt warmth spreading through her body.

Wordlessly he slipped his hands upward from her waist until they cupped the swelling fullness of her breasts. His touch was muted by the robe, soft and sensual as he explored her. Cathlyn's hands closed over his powerful shoulder muscles, and with the very tip of her tongue she teased the sensitive hollow at the base of his throat. She felt him tense, and when he pulled her to him, the entire length of his body was hard against her softness.

Marc held her for a few moments, and then, without explanation, he said, "Come with me." He grabbed her hand, and she followed him out of the kitchen and down a hallway. He opened the door to a large bathroom.

Cathlyn stopped in the doorway and stared. Mirrors covered one entire wall and the ceiling. The other walls were papered in a deep, vibrant red. A black vanity stretched to a lacquered Oriental screen, which apparently shielded the commode. Across the room was a black sunken tub, gracefully curved. "This is the sexiest bathroom I've ever seen!" she exclaimed in amazement.

Marc laughed. "I kind of like it. I thought the whirlpool might feel really good." He turned the brass faucets, and steaming water poured into the tub.

"You mean we're going in there?"

"You'll love it," he assured her, loosening the belt on her robe in one deft motion.

"Have you got any bubble bath?" she asked with a wicked twinkle in her eye.

"Bubble bath?" He sounded startled.

"Bubble bath," she repeated. Then she saw the gleam in his eye.

"Wait just a minute." While he rummaged through the vanity cabinet, Cathlyn disappeared behind the Oriental screen. When she emerged, the tub was filled with clouds of white bubbles, and Marc was nowhere to be seen.

Slipping out of her robe, she let her body sink into the warm, swirling water until she was buried in bubbles up to her chin. She leaned luxuriously against the curve of the tub, which was warm against her back. This is sheer luxury, she thought lazily.

When Marc reappeared, he was holding two crystal goblets. "For you," he said with a flourish, handing her a goblet of white wine poured over tiny pieces of cracked ice. He let his robe drop to the floor behind him and stepped lithely over the wide rim of the tub. His body disappeared beneath bubbles up to his shoulders, but below the water she could feel his firmly muscled thigh against her leg.

"To us"—he grinned, holding his drink toward her—"and to a wonderful, decadent weekend."

"And what makes you think I'll drink to that?" she asked demurely.

He donned a sober expression, all except for the sparkle in his hazel eyes. "Because I'll bury you in bubbles if you don't," he told her solemnly.

The tinkling of ice mixed with her laughter as

she drank the toast. Setting her glass on the rim of the tub, she said threateningly, "Unless I get you first." She puffed out her cheeks and blew hard, sending bubbles flying at him.

"You just wait," he said with a laugh. He scooped up a mound of bubbles and left a frothy white handprint in her hair. She flung handfuls of bubbles back while the whirlpool swirled water over their naked bodies. Finally he grabbed her, crushing a mountain of bubbles between them as they came together. His hand stroked her thigh, moving upward along her curves while his tongue followed the sensuous lines of her mouth.

"Oh, Marc," she moaned softly, "I can't believe this." Her hands explored his slippery body. Enveloped with him in the never-ceasing flow of the water, all her doubts were swept away.

"Cathlyn, I want you," he whispered, his voice hoarse and heavy.

She held her breath, waiting, as when a great symphony enters its final crescendo, waiting when he stopped to stroke her softness, waiting for what seemed like forever, gripped by seething passion longing to burst free.

"Marc," she cried out. She pressed her head back against the edge of the tub, arching her body upward to meet him.

Then she heard his soft groan and nothing more. She was aware of the water, which seemed to swirl faster and faster, and all at once she was inside a raging whirlpool of heat. The explosions came one after another, as brilliant as the flashing mirrors above them.

When it was over, she lay limply against him, sheltered in his arms, the gently flowing water caressing her skin. Closing her eyes, she sighed softly, resting her head on his shoulder as she floated in a sea of happiness.

"I can't imagine life without you," he murmured into her ear as he gently teased wet strands of her hair into place. "You are the loveliest, most passionate woman I've ever known. I want to build a future with you, Cathlyn," he added softly.

His words brought reality flooding back, and stirred a flash of uncertainty in her. "I love you . . ." she began tentatively.

Marc heard the hesitation in her voice. "What's past is past," he told her firmly, and then leaned down to kiss her lips. "We have to put that behind us."

"I'll try," she promised, knowing that saying the words might be a whole lot easier than whatever lay ahead.

Chapter Seven

AS THE WEEKS PASSED, spring ripened into summer. A hot, steamy Chicago summer. The intense sun radiated from the skyscrapers that enclosed the city like the walls of an oven. The pavement below absorbed the heat, then reflected it back in invisible waves. Each afternoon when Cathlyn left her office and walked across the street to get her car, the narrow heels of her pumps would sink into the soft, sticky asphalt.

"At this rate I'm not going to have a decent pair of shoes left to wear," she complained to Marc late one afternoon over wine spritzers in her apartment. She either saw Marc or talked to him nearly every day, and happy hour on Fridays, whether at home or as a prelude to a leisurely dinner out, had become one of their valued rituals.

"It's so damn hot," he agreed. "I was going to take you to the ball game tomorrow, but I don't know whether it's worth it."

"Unless the temperature drops at least twenty degrees, I won't even discuss it," Cathlyn declared. She smiled at him. She had been to more ball games and concerts in the park, and gone for more walks by the lake with Marc, than in all her previous years in Chicago.

Last week they'd spent a magnificent evening at the symphony and stopped at a gala party afterward. It was their first venture into Marc's world with all its glitter and society types. For Cathlyn it stirred memories of her childhood that she'd have preferred to leave buried. She'd always hated big, noisy parties, and at the beginning this one had seemed like all the rest. But with Marc's light, protective hand on her shoulder and his full attention focused on her, this party hadn't been so bad. Everyone there seemed to know Marc, and they all were anxious to meet her. She'd immediately liked several of Marc's friends. When it was over, she had to admit that thinking about going had been worse than actually doing it.

She enjoyed the party a lot more than the day they'd had lunch at Rive Gauche, a lunch Marc jokingly said he owed her after their previous fiasco. While they were eating, they were interrupted four times by acquaintances of Marc's who'd stopped by the table. Afterward Cathlyn confided that the lunch didn't begin to measure up to their picnic by the lake, and he had agreed with her.

Cathlyn watched Marc drain his wine spritzer. He put down his glass and stood up abruptly. "I feel like I'm in a box with the air-conditioning on," he complained, "and I know exactly what we're going to do about it. Grab your bikini and come on."

"Marc, I don't really want to swim," Cathlyn protested wearily.

"We're not going to swim," Marc announced, pulling her to her feet. "We're going to sail. If we hurry, we can get to Belmont Harbor in time to catch my brother and his wife before they cast off. They go out every Friday night."

Cathlyn's response was immediate. "Sailing? Now that would be fun." Her blue eyes sparkled with anticipation as she headed toward the bedroom to change her clothes. "But are you sure it's all right for us to just show up?" she called out to him.

"Of course," Marc assured her. "Hurry up," he prodded.

"I am hurrying," Cathlyn insisted, quickly pulling a pair of shorts over her bikini.

"You haven't met Andy's wife, have you?" Marc asked as she reappeared in the living room.

"No," Cathlyn said, suddenly cautious. "What's she like?" She'd already met Andy, and she liked him. But somehow she'd conjured up an impression of his wife that revolved around cool perfection and little tea sandwiches.

"Buffie?" Marc considered her question. "She's attractive, well put together. She suits Andrew. She's been pushing to have us to dinner for weeks," he added. "I just haven't found time when I was willing to share you." He gave her a quick kiss that sent tremors through her. "And I wouldn't tonight if it weren't so damn hot," he added.

Less than half an hour later Marc and Cathlyn dashed across the grassy strip separating the harbor parking lot from the boat dock.

"I haven't sailed in years," Cathlyn confessed breathlessly, tying the tail of her plaid gauze shirt tighter across the top of the sleek white shorts that covered her bikini. "What kind of a boat is it?"

"A thirty-eight-foot sloop," Marc replied. "Usually we race her, but we've both been too busy this summer."

"We used to have a boat," Cathlyn reminisced, taking three steps for every two of Marc's to keep up with him. It was one of the pleasant memories of her childhood. "But I never was a very good sailor," she added.

"So long as you keep your head down and your body in the boat, we'll handle the rest," Marc assured her.

"Sounds like you think you're pretty good," she teased him.

"The best, of course." He took her hand and led her to the weathered wooden dock. They wound their way quickly along row after row of yachts, sailboats, and giant inboards. Laughter and music from on-board parties filled the heavy July air.

Cathlyn caught sight of Andrew Harrison standing at the helm of a majestic sloop, ready to start the engine he would use to maneuver out of the harbor.

"Hey, wait for us," Marc shouted to his brother.

Cathlyn's eyes were on the boat. Beneath its towering masts, with sails still furled, the hull was stark white. Its sleek lines stood out from the other boats in the harbor like a Mercedes on a street lined with station wagons.

"Marc!" Andrew waved back, watching them approach. "And Cathlyn. Glad to see you. Come on aboard. A couple of minutes more and you'd have missed us. Why didn't you have the harbor-master let me know you were coming?"

"The thought never crossed my mind, big brother." Marc grinned, throwing an armload of towels and jackets into the cockpit. He vaulted lightly over the gunwale and reached across the water for Cathlyn's hand to help her on board. The boat swayed slightly as she jumped down into the cockpit.

"Yes, Marc," seconded another voice through the hatchway. "If you'd have let me know, I'd have picked up the smoked oysters and anchovies."

Cathlyn watched a tall, slender woman with frosted blond hair emerge from the cabin. She wore a trim white pique cover-up that exposed about three inches of a dark purple swimsuit. Her gold bracelets sparkled in the fading sunlight.

"Oh," the woman said, stopping in surprise, "you must be Cathlyn. I'm Elizabeth Harrison, but please call me Buffie." She extended her hand.

Cathlyn returned the warm, firm grasp. Buffie Harrison looked exactly the way Cathlyn had expected. "I'm delighted to meet you," she responded automatically.

"Welcome to the *Sea Sprite,*" Buffie said effusively. "Just make yourself right at home."

"Why don't you two settle yourselves while Andy and I get under way?" Marc suggested, nodding toward the narrow benches along the sides of the cockpit. "Careful of the boom," he warned. Buff and Cathlyn ducked to avoid being hit.

"Marc tells me you're a psychologist," Buffie began, motioning for Cathlyn to sit on the bench beside her. "I understand you work with the girls at Angel House."

"Yes, I do volunteer a great deal of my time there," Cathlyn answered.

"Marc said he's been out there several times,"

Buffie continued. The comment was innocuous, but the tone of her voice put Cathlyn on guard.

"Yes," Cathlyn affirmed, less at ease than before. "He often comes with me." She glanced up at Marc, who stood on the bow, the wind blowing his hair. The boat engine growled softly as Andrew maneuvered them out of the harbor.

"I can't quite imagine him out on the West Side working with a bunch of homeless girls," Buffie remarked. "That's not his style."

"Why do you say that?" Cathlyn kept her voice carefully controlled, aware that she was about to confront the schism between the two Marc Harrisons. "He seems to fit right in."

"I suppose anything's possible." Buffie laughed. "He's always been a party boy. He likes to have fun."

"Maybe he's found a different way to have fun," Cathlyn flipped back with cool assurance in her voice. Inside, her stomach was churning. This woman knew Marc well, and she had known him for a long time. She hadn't spoken unkindly, just frankly, and that shook Cathlyn's confidence. What if Buffie were right?

Andrew cut the engine, and a silence settled around them, broken only by the wind and the intermittent cries of the birds. Again Cathlyn looked at Marc standing on the bow, his muscles straining as he raised the flapping jib. He balanced easily, his taut thigh muscles bulging below his dark green swim trunks. His print shirt, of the same dark green that flecked his eyes, was unbuttoned, and flapped in the lake breeze. Cathlyn could see tiny beads of perspiration glisten on the dark, tightly curled hair on his chest. Shoving her sunglasses up on her head, she caught Marc's admiring glance and smiled up at him. But inside, the questions lingered. Was she kidding herself? Was she going to find out one of these days that she only thought she knew him?

Buffie interrupted her thoughts. "Tell me more about Angel House," she said, tilting her head toward the late-afternoon sun. "The Junior League has gathered up clothes for them for years. Are they federally funded, or do they have a foundation?"

Cathlyn stared at her for a moment before she answered. "Neither one," she replied slowly. She realized it would be almost impossible for Buffie Harrison to conceive of the hand-to-mouth operation Tom and Jean ran.

"How do they manage?" Buffie inquired curiously.

Cathlyn shrugged. "Lots of love and some private contributions. It's hard sometimes."

"I should think so," Buffie remarked. "They need more than that."

Cathlyn didn't answer. There was no point in trying to explain it to Buffie. She looked back at Marc, who was securing the jib with a few twists around the cleat. He was lithe and sure, like a lifelong sailor, which, Cathlyn realized, he probably was. He had shed his shoes and shirt, and was wearing nothing but his swim trunks. The summer sun had turned his skin a deep bronze. Suddenly she wanted very much to go to him and lose herself in the sanctuary of his arms.

Picking up the wind off starboard, the sails billowed and the boat heeled slightly. Marc leaned into the wind as he moved lightly across the deck to the cockpit. "What did I tell you?" he beamed at Cathlyn. "Isn't this great? Really nice and cool."

"Magnificent," Cathlyn agreed, looking up into his eyes.

"See, Marc," interjected Buffie, "we've been trying to tell you all summer what you're missing." She turned to Cathlyn. "Maybe you can get him to come along more often. Otherwise I'm the crew, and my hands are going to turn to leather before fall."

"Ah, an ulterior motive," Marc teased, settling next to Cathlyn on the narrow bench.

Andrew joined them, flinging his arm around Buffie. "Woman," he said to her with a grin, "see if you can conjure up some drinks."

"Aye, aye, sir," Buffie replied with a back-handed salute before she disappeared into the cabin.

Buffie Harrison was a type, Cathlyn thought: one of the North Shore elite who probably played lots of tennis, gave perfect parties, and raised perfect children who invariably got over being perfect at age fifteen, which was when Cathlyn usually met them. She closed her eyes, leaning back to let the wind whip her hair and cool her skin in the heat of early evening. Cathlyn had known lots of these cool, confident women with their successful husbands and their big houses, women who raced through their busy lives with the specter of boredom driving them on. Surely Marc wouldn't expect her to be like Buffie, she thought. And yet that was the prototype. She was his brother's wife. A shiver ran through Cathlyn.

Aware of Marc beside her on the bench, Cathlyn moved a little closer to him. His thigh, wet from the spray, felt cold against her skin but stirred warmth inside her. Buffie reappeared with a tray of tall frosty drinks, and Cathlyn took a long, slow sip. "Mmmm, good," she murmured as Marc slipped his arm around her.

Buffie handed Andrew his drink and settled herself on the bench across from them. "I've been trying to get Cathlyn to tell me about Angel House, but we keep getting interrupted," she explained to Marc and Andrew. "She says they need money."

Cathlyn frowned almost imperceptibly. Angel House? Here they were, flying across the waves, a fine mist from the spray cooling them, the wind in their hair. Why would Buffie keep talking about Angel House?

Andrew seemed to have the answer. "Buff," he warned sternly, "I can see your wheels turning. You're about to make that orphanage into your pet project for the season. Just lean back and enjoy the scenery."

Cathlyn didn't follow him. "What do you mean?"

"Buff is the social-action chairman for the Winnetka Junior League, and she can get very involved in fund-raising," Andrew explained fondly.

"Fund-raising?" Suddenly Cathlyn understood, and her wheels were beginning to turn as well.

"Exactly what are Angel House's most pressing financial needs?" Buffie asked.

"I can answer that," Marc interjected. "What those girls need is a recreation room. They need space to spread out, some place to have some fun."

"They also need more bathrooms," Cathlyn added.

"True," Marc agreed. "There's always a line to use the facilities."

Cathlyn laughed, remembering their last visit to Angel House when Marc queued up with several of the girls, patiently awaiting his turn.

"Three or four bathrooms and a rec room—that doesn't sound like much of a problem," Buffie noted. She tapped her manicured nails on the edge of the bench. Her eyes narrowed, and Cathlyn could almost see the thoughts snapping into place.

"We can have an art auction," she proclaimed, as though she had been planning it for weeks. "A spectacular art auction." She turned to Marc. "All right, Mr. Architect, how much money does the Junior League have to raise?"

Marc gazed steadily at his sister-in-law. "Shoot at a hundred thousand dollars. If there's any extra, we can do some decorating."

Cathlyn stared at him. He was treating the idea like an established fact.

"That's a pretty tall order, even for the Junior League," Andrew remarked.

"It is way beyond anything we've ever tried before," Buffie admitted. "But we might be able to do it, and if a certain architect was willing to donate his time . . ."

"You know I will," Marc confirmed.

Cathlyn looked from one to the other. They were obviously serious. "Never in a million years would Jean and Tommy even dream about anything like this. . . ." Cathlyn paused and looked Buffie directly in the eye. "Do you really think you can raise the money?"

"Are you willing to present the plan at my next Junior League meeting, give a talk and maybe a slide presentation?" Buffie countered.

Cathlyn hesitated. The last thing she wanted to do was get involved in a meeting of the Junior League. And yet how could she say no if it were for Angel House? She took a deep breath. "If that's what it takes, I'll do it," she agreed.

"That's the spirit," Marc pronounced, giving her a hug. She wondered if he knew how she felt.

"Refill the drinks," Andrew ordered, "and we'll toast the Angel House Art Auction."

"To take place in November at the new Continental Hotel," added Buffie.

Cathlyn watched Buffie gather the glasses on a Plexiglas tray and disappear into the cabin. Done, they'd agreed, just like that. Cathlyn shook her head. Now Marc and his brother were talking about buying a new sail, and Buffie was getting more drinks and probably whipping up hors d'oeuvres. She couldn't quite get a handle on Buffie. She wasn't the kind of woman Cathlyn was drawn to, and yet there was a directness about her that was refreshing. Besides, Cathlyn realized, it would be hard to dislike someone who had just committed herself to a major project on behalf of Angel House.

Later, when she and Marc were stretched out on the deck, Cathlyn found herself still thinking about the auction. It seemed an enormous undertaking to settle in a casual conversation one evening on a boat. "Marc," she asked, "do you think this fund-raiser of Buffie's will really get off the ground?"

"Of course," Marc reassured her with a kiss on the nose. "Buff is practically a professional fund-raiser. I don't know why I never thought of turning her loose on Angel House before." He propped himself on his elbow and looked at Cathlyn. "You seem to get along pretty well with Buffie," he observed.

"She wasn't exactly what I expected," Cathlyn admitted.

"What did you expect?"

"I don't know," Cathlyn mused. Someone artificial and uncaring? And, if so, why? she questioned herself silently. Generalizations like that were unfair, and she knew it. Buffie's approach wasn't like hers, but in its own way it was equally valid. Cathlyn shook her head. She was beginning to suspect that her problems with people like Buffie Harrison had more to do with herself than with them.

The sun, a glowing ball of red filmed with Chicago's ever-present haze, hung low against the skyline. Cathlyn settled back and gazed at the sky, fading from brilliant azure to the deep purple of evening. Marc silently took her hand, and she lay quietly against him, not wanting to think anymore. She was vaguely aware that the light breeze had begun to pick up, skimming the tops off the waves in billows of white.

Marc was aware of it too. "Wind's picking up," he noted casually. "Probably about time for us to head in. Did you have a good time?"

Cathlyn rubbed her cheek against his bare shoulder. "I always have a good time when I'm with you," she answered.

Marc let his hand slide across the curve of her hip and rest lightly on her thigh. "It doesn't matter what we do, does it," he said softly, "as long as we're together." He leaned across and kissed her.

Cathlyn opened her lips slightly to meet his, reveling in the sensation that washed over her at his touch. They'd grown together in so many ways over these last months, she thought, slowly letting those thoughts give way to feelings. Then the boat lurched, heeling toward starboard, and both Cathlyn and Marc snapped back abruptly.

"Hey, Marc," called Andy from the cockpit. "Don't get so busy that you forget to sail. Time to head in, or we're going to have a rough ride home. We should have been in an hour ago."

"Turn on the running lights," Marc yelled back, never taking his eyes from Cathlyn. He took Cathlyn's hand as they stood up, leaning against a stanchion to steady them. "Want to help me with the jib?" he asked her.

"Sure," she agreed. "What do I do?"

"Loosen the sheet and let her down slowly,"

Marc instructed. "I'll haul the sail in and secure it."

Cathlyn did as he directed, but nothing happened. Marc tugged at the sail but also got no response.

"Damn thing's hung up," he called back to Andy. "Where's the boat hook?"

The heavy white sail was just loose enough that it snapped and filled with wind. The boat rolled menacingly.

"Hold on, Cathlyn," Marc yelled at her. "It's rough out here."

Cathlyn nodded. She knelt down, holding fast to an anchor cleat to keep herself from being pitched across the rolling bow. She was uneasy but not frightened. Both men seemed to know exactly what they were doing. Marc had unlatched the boat hook and begun working on the stubborn jib. The boat rocked, and Cathlyn looked down to see the whitecapped waves pounding hard against the hull. Floating debris churned in the darkening water. Then she looked more closely. A dark, menacing object loomed directly in line with the bow.

"Marc," she cried in alarm. "There's something in the water."

Marc looked quickly over his shoulder, and he immediately saw it too. "Andy," he yelled, "log dead ahead—it's a big one."

Andrew lost no time. "Hang on, everybody," he shouted.

Even as he spoke, Cathlyn saw the boom begin to move. Then it snapped hard across the cockpit and the boat lunged, heeling almost at a right angle to the rising black water. Cathlyn pitched forward, still clutching the cleat with both hands to keep herself from being thrown into the mast. She held on, sprawled belly-down on the deck. Suddenly Marc cried out. She watched, helpless, as he skidded across the wet deck and slammed against the lifelines. For a brief instant she thought he was all right. Then he catapulted over the lines, plummeting out of sight into the angry black water.

"Marc!" Cathlyn cried out, scrambling to her feet. "Marc, where are you?" She slid across the wet deck, grabbing for a stanchion, still yelling Marc's name. The boat was moving, carrying them away from where he'd gone overboard.

"Marc!" she heard Andrew's voice echo his name. "Do you see him?"

Frantically Cathlyn scanned the surface of the water. It was black and hostile and empty. She could see the log rolling across the waves. "No, no, I don't see him!" she shouted. "We've got to go back!" she screamed into the wind. She could feel Andy struggling to bring the boat around.

A thousand thoughts shot through her mind. What if Marc had hit his head? What if he hadn't surfaced? What if he was lost out there and they couldn't get to him in time? "My God, no!" she cried out. Then she saw something else, lighter in color. "Wait, maybe I do see him," she called to Andy. Was it Marc? In the rapidly engulfing darkness, she couldn't be sure. "Marc, answer me!" she screamed, leaning closer to the water. *Quickly,* she thought. *I've got to act quickly.*

"Cathlyn, don't do it," she heard Andy yell, as

though he knew what was in her mind. But she had to do it. She had to try. With a single thrust she arched over the lifelines and plunged into the dark, stormy lake.

The icy water closed over her, and she struggled against it, kicking hard. After what seemed an eternity, she surfaced, her lungs bursting. But a wave broke over her, submerging her again. Doggedly she fought her way back up, gasping for breath. This time she stayed afloat, treading water so that she bobbed up and down with the rhythm of the waves.

Her body screamed with cold. She looked in vain for Marc, but in the darkness, all she could see were the running lights of the boat. Fear overwhelmed her, a terrible fear for Marc and for herself. Her body was numb with cold, and although she was a strong swimmer, the water was stronger.

"Marc," she shouted, "where are you?" But her voice blew away in the wind. She heard the roar of the outboard starting and knew Andy was bringing the boat back to them. Or to her. How were they going to find Marc?

She didn't hear him come to her. It wasn't until his strong arm circled her that she knew he was there. At the instant of recognition a prayer of thanksgiving escaped her icy blue lips. "Thank God!" she murmured, resting back against him. "Thank God."

Her relief paled against his blaze of anger. "Cathlyn, what the hell do you think you're doing?" he demanded roughly.

"Saving you!" she yelled back, spitting out a mouthful of water.

"Dammit, Cathlyn," he roared at her. "You could have been killed."

"So could you," she shouted at him, her teeth chattering from fear and cold. "What was I supposed to do, let you drown?"

"One of us would be a damn sight better than both of us," he growled, gripping her shoulder hard as his powerful legs kicked rhythmically, supporting them in the waves.

"Marc! Cathlyn!" Andy and Buffie's voices echoed across the water, calling their names.

"Andy, over here!" Marc yelled back, waving one arm high over his head.

The lights of the boat grew brighter, and slowly Andy pulled alongside. "Life ring coming out," he hollered.

Cathlyn heard a whizzing sound, and the white ring landed in the water in front of them. Marc grabbed it and placed Cathlyn's hands firmly over the edge. "Don't you dare let go!" he commanded roughly. He swam around behind her, encircling her body with his own as he reached around her to anchor them both to the ring. "We're ready," he shouted to Andrew. "Bring us in."

"Coming in," Andrew acknowledged. The ring jerked as Andrew pulled the rope taut and began hauling them in. The waves slapped viciously, and Cathlyn felt her whole body shaking, even with Marc's warmth all around her. With a final tug Andrew pulled the life ring against the side of the boat, and Marc reached across to grab the portable ladder his brother had hung over the side.

"Can you make it?" Andrew called down with concern as Marc guided Cathlyn toward the ladder.

"I'm fine," Cathlyn responded, finding the bottom step with her foot and willing her body not to shake so hard. Marc clasped one hand firmly at her waist and held the ladder with the other hand to steady it as she climbed. When she was safely in the boat, he pulled himself up behind her, swinging over the gunwale in a single, fluid motion.

"I thought for a minute there that we might have lost you," Andy said, handing them both thick terry towels to wrap up in. He embraced his brother roughly.

"No such luck," Marc responded flippantly. But he clapped Andy on the shoulder, and Cathlyn could feel the bond between them.

"You are both absolutely freezing," Buffie scolded. "Hurry into the cabin and dry off. You'll find some clothes in the upper compartments."

"Go ahead," Andy seconded. "We'll take the boat in."

"Good plan." Marc guided Cathlyn toward the small enclosure. Once inside, he quickly peeled off her wet bikini and began to rub her nude body briskly with a terry towel. She was so cold, her skin was blue. As he rubbed her, she felt prickly sensations in her shaking limbs. It was several minutes before her mind cleared enough for her to realize that Marc was still in his trunks, his wet hair dripping.

"Stop," she said. "You're as cold as I am."

"Nothing warms me up faster than rubbing you," he teased, sliding his hand playfully under the towel.

"Oh, brrr, your fingers are like ice." She pulled away from him.

"Fine response that is," he retorted, draping one towel around her shoulders and using the other to dry himself. "But at least you're coming back to life. Let's see if we can find those clothes Buff was talking about." He opened the small doors above the built-in couch and rummaged briefly before pulling out two warm-up suits, one pink and gray, the other a dark burgundy.

"Oh, do those look good." Cathlyn shivered inside the damp towel.

"Now, let's get you into this," Marc said, holding up the gray pants to find the front. He lifted each of her feet in turn and pushed them into the heavy fleece pants, which he deftly pulled up to her waist.

"You don't have to dress me," she protested.

"But I like to," he declared, lifting one end of the towel from her shoulder. He paused, leaning over to kiss her. "There are lots of ways to warm up," he observed, removing the towel completely.

"There sure are," Cathlyn agreed, shivering again, but not with cold. She raised her arms so Marc could drop the gray-and-pink sweatshirt over her head. "Now do something about you," she directed, feeling the beginnings of warmth seep through her.

Quickly he stripped off his swim trunks and

pulled on the other warm-up suit. Then he took Cathlyn in his arms. "Don't you ever, ever pull a stunt like that again," he ordered, burying his face in her wet hair.

"I didn't want you to drown," she said defensively.

"So naturally you jumped in after me so we could both drown," he murmured into her ear. "That's real logic at work." He caressed her lips with his, settling slowly into a deep kiss that stirred longing in Cathlyn.

Pressing her body against his, she tipped her head back and looked directly into his eyes. "If I'd been the one swept overboard and you couldn't find me, what would you have done?"

He stared at her for a long moment, drinking in the intensity in those deep blue eyes. He couldn't believe that this fragile creature had leapt into the water to save his life. It was a damn fool stunt that showed she didn't have a lick of common sense. It also told him something else. Cathlyn was deeply in love with him. She'd have to be in order to do something that insane. His arms tightened around her possessively. "You're incredible, Cathlyn Tate," he answered softly.

"I'm also cold," she said in a small voice, snuggling against him.

"When I get you home, I'm going to warm you up properly," he promised, caressing the curve of her breast through the soft fleece.

"Mmm," Cathlyn answered. "I hope it's soon." The ordeal in the water faded as she stood locked in his arms.

Chapter Eight

"AH . . . AHH-CHOO." Cathlyn reached for a pink tissue to blow her nose and pulled the quilt more snugly around her shoulders. "Don't you dare get near me," she warned Marc, who was sitting on the edge of the bed.

"You didn't feel that way last night," he reminded her, and she wiggled slightly under the covers.

"I didn't know I had a cold then," she retorted. "I was so close to frozen, I couldn't feel anything—" She stopped, realizing what she had said.

"Sure seemed to me like you felt a whole lot." Marc chuckled, trailing his fingers suggestively along her cheek.

"I mean, until I warmed up," Cathlyn retorted, burying her head in the pillow. "Anyway, today I know I have a drippy, awful cold, and I absolutely don't want you to catch it," she announced firmly. As if to make her point more forcefully, she sneezed again, several times in succession.

"I never catch colds," Marc asserted, nuzzling Cathlyn's neck. "Haven't had one since I was a kid."

"And you're not going to get one now, at least not if I have anything to say about it." She struggled under the covers. "Marc, stop kissing me."

"I'm not anywhere near your mouth," he declared, feathering a line of soft kisses around her ear.

"You know perfectly well that my skin is literally alive with viruses just waiting to attack you," Cathlyn insisted. With enormous difficulty she squirmed away from him. "Here, take a vitamin C," she ordered, handing Marc the bottle. "Just in case."

"In case of what?" Marc asked her, eyeing the small white tablets with suspicion.

"In case you have any cold viruses in your system," Cathlyn explained. Wearily she burrowed under the quilt and closed her eyes. "Now go away and don't come back until I'm well," she murmured sleepily.

"You couldn't possibly recover properly without my help," Marc replied. "Besides, if I hadn't kept you warm after your little swim last night, you'd probably have double pneumonia instead of a common cold."

Cathlyn forced her eyes open partway and tried to glare at him. "Go away," she repeated.

"These vitamin C pills are useless," Marc continued, setting the bottle on the nightstand in disgust. "What you really need is chicken soup."

"Right." Cathlyn closed her eyes again and rolled over.

Marc leaned down and kissed her on the cheek. "Sleep tight, sweetheart," he whispered softly. "I'll take care of everything."

Very quietly, so that he wouldn't awaken Cathlyn, Marc stood up and left the bedroom, closing the door softly behind him. He headed directly for the kitchen, whistling a jaunty tune as he walked. Cathlyn really did need some chicken soup, he thought. It would be a simple matter to phone the deli and have some delivered.

As he reached for the phone, an inspiration struck him. He would make Cathlyn some homemade chicken soup. Homemade had to be better than anything he could buy, and the savory aroma in the apartment would help clear her head. Marc glanced around the compact kitchen. There wasn't a cookbook in sight. Then he remembered. Cathlyn practically lived on cottage cheese and carrots when she was alone. Probably doesn't have much need for a cookbook, he thought.

He reached for the phone again and rang up Jones. This sort of thing was his department. Five minutes later, with a superb chicken-soup recipe stuffed in his shirt pocket, Marc was on his way to the supermarket to purchase a plump stewing hen. He was very pleased with himself.

Several hours later Cathlyn opened her eyes and groaned. Turning over, she checked the clock. She groaned again. She knew it wasn't possible, but she felt even worse than before her nap. Miserably, she blew her nose, throwing the tissue on the overflowing mound in her white wicker wastebasket. She was reaching for the box of throat lozenges on her bedside table when Marc burst through the door with a tray in his hands.

"I thought you went home," she said, trying to stifle her feelings of relief that he hadn't.

"Of course I didn't go home," he retorted. "I am going to make you well, and I've got something here that's going to do the trick." He set the tray on Cathlyn's white lacquered dresser before walking to the bed and leaning down to kiss her on the forehead.

"Marc—" she protested.

"I know, I know," he responded impatiently. "Now come on, sit up." He lifted her by the shoulders and plumped the pillows behind her.

Cathlyn skeptically eyed the steaming porcelain bowl in the center of the tray. "I'm not hungry," she croaked hoarsely.

"This is not food," Marc asserted, picking up the tray. "It is the one sure, certain cure-all cold remedy endorsed by every mother since the beginning of time." He set the tray on her lap and began spooning hot chicken soup into her mouth. "Isn't it great?" he asked enthusiastically.

"It *is* pretty good," Cathlyn admitted, taking the spoon from his hand. "Where did you find it?" She took another bite, wiping the dribbles from her chin with the napkin Marc had neatly folded on the tray. "I don't usually keep canned soup on the shelves."

"You don't keep much of anything on the shelves," Marc observed.

"Then where did this come from?" Cathlyn persisted in a raspy voice.

"I made it," Marc answered nonchalantly.

"You made it?" Cathlyn's eyes opened wider. "From scratch?" She noticed the red-checked dish towel slung around his waist like an apron.

"From scratch," Marc confirmed. "Starting with the finest stewing hen available in the entire city of Chicago—well, at least at the local supermarket."

"You cooked a chicken?" Cathlyn still couldn't quite picture it.

"Simmered," Marc corrected, "with carrots, celery, onion, and a hint of poultry seasoning."

Cathlyn stared at him. Only yesterday Buffie had suggested that Marc was a flashy playboy with nothing more serious on his mind than long-legged show girls and the trendiest place in town to be seen. Today this so-called playboy had turned domestic and brewed a pot of homemade chicken soup in her kitchen. Would she ever figure out Marc Harrison?

For the next two days, until Cathlyn was back on her feet, Marc stayed with her, sleeping unhappily on the couch at her insistence to avoid catching her cold. As she lay in bed listening to him whistle while he cleaned the kitchen, or watching him as he tenderly smoothed the quilt over her, Cathlyn pondered their growing closeness. It was impossible for her to believe that Marc was anything other than this warm, funny, compassionate man she knew. Oh, yes, he was powerful and self-assured. And he certainly was intensely passionate when they made love. No question of that, Cathlyn thought, smiling to herself, remembering.

By the second evening, Cathlyn was showing marked improvement after all of the tender, loving care she had received. Marc sat on the edge of the bed as he had so often during those two days, sometimes talking to her, sometimes reading to her. "I think you're going to live," he announced, looking her over carefully.

"My nose is still red," she complained, touching it gingerly with her finger.

"But not as red," he assured her as he took her hand. "Even your voice is beginning to sound like you instead of that sexy frog I've been conversing with," he added, moving nearer to her.

"Now wait a minute," she warned. "Better is not the same as cured."

"Close enough," Marc pronounced, taking her in his arms.

"Marc, stop," she protested, wiggling against him. "You've been really good up till now, but I might still be contagious and—"

"If you want me to stay good, stop wiggling against me that way."

"I am not wiggling," she protested, shifting her weight again. "If you'd sit over in the chair where you belong, it wouldn't be a problem, anyway."

Marc leaned down and took off his shoes. In a quick motion he pulled back the quilt and climbed in beside Cathlyn. "Actually," he said, "this is where I belong."

"What do you think you're doing?"

"You know exactly what I'm doing," he answered. He traced the neckline of her nightgown with the tip of his finger barely touching her skin, stopping to toy with the satin ribbon that held the neck closed. "And you like it as much as I do," he whispered.

Cathlyn felt her body quiver, and she willed it to stop. She loved to have him touch her. "Marc," she protested, "you promised!" She tried to make her objection vehement, but she knew she wasn't very successful. The danger of Marc's catching her cold was less and less important. She could feel his body pressed against hers, warm and inviting even through the soft flannel of her gown.

Gently he tugged at one end of the ribbon until the bow was gone and the flannel pulled aside. "Of course, I don't want you to get chilled," he said, bending his head to blow a line of playful kisses along the exposed skin.

"I don't think we're going to have to worry about that," Cathlyn breathed. All thoughts of resistance had vanished, and when she felt his mouth on hers, she opened her lips to welcome him.

As he kissed her, his hand slid down inside her gown. He knew her body so well now that his every touch produced delicious sensations. Cathlyn stroked his chest with her fingertips, searching for his shirt buttons. She began at the top and unfastened them one by one, until his chest was bare.

"I think I like that," he told her, lying back on the mountain of pillows. "And I know I like you," he added, and then drew in a sharp breath when she opened the snap on his jeans with a tug. She undressed him slowly, touching him in response to his soft moans of pleasure.

He reached up to slip her nightgown over her head and toss it aside before he clasped his hands around her hips and brought her back to him. They moved in perfect harmony, the bond between them all-encompassing.

"Now, Cathlyn," he whispered urgently.

"Yes, now." Together they swirled into the moment of total ecstasy.

All sense of time was gone when she opened her eyes. It didn't seem that she had slept, but she wasn't sure. She watched Marc, still partially beneath her, his head sharing her pillow, his eyes closed peacefully. She loved him so much. Her mind wandered back to that awful moment on the boat when she had shouted his name into the darkness but heard only the pounding of the water in reply. What if she had lost him? The possibility was almost more than she could consider.

She stroked his shoulder, still thinking about that night. Everyone had been angry at her for going into the water—Marc, Buffie, and Andrew—and yet she knew if she had it to do over again, nothing would change. As much as she valued common sense, sometimes there were things you had to do. Things outside the realm of reason. Slowly she reached her hand down until she found the edge of the quilt and drew it across their naked bodies. She let her eyes slip shut. Tomorrow it would be time to face the world again. But tonight she could be with him.

When Marc called her the next afternoon, he sneezed twice during the conversation, which didn't surprise Cathlyn at all. "Take your vitamin C," she warned him.

"No chance," he scoffed. "Quit being an alarmist."

When Marc didn't call the following day, Cathlyn was mildly surprised but so caught up with the backlog of work that had accumulated while she was sick, she didn't do anything about it. That evening, after eating a mushroom omelet which she noted ruefully was not as good as the ones Marc made, she picked up the phone.

"Mr. Harrison left instructions that he is quite busy with a project and not to be disturbed," Jones reported in a businesslike tone.

Cathlyn hesitated. She knew Marc was deeply involved in developing a proposal for a shopping mall and that the days he had spent nursing her had no doubt thrown him behind schedule. Still, something made her suspicious.

"Are you sure he included me in those instructions?" she queried Jones.

"Yes, Miss Tate," Jones replied. "He specifically said he was not to be disturbed under any circumstances."

"Has he ever said that before?" Cathlyn asked.

"Not that I recall," Jones answered.

"Jones," Cathlyn began patiently, "I want the truth. I understand that you must abide by Mr. Harrison's instructions. However, I want to know: Is Mr. Harrison in bed with a miserable, drippy cold?"

For the first time since she'd met him, Cathlyn heard Jones hesitate. "Well . . ." he said.

"That's what I thought," she replied. "And I assume you've already prepared the chicken soup?"

"Most assuredly," Jones answered.

"Good. Tell Mr. Harrison I'll be right over. On second thought, don't tell him anything. That way he can't object."

For the next week Cathlyn kept Marc supplied with boxes of pink tissues and a steady diet of vitamin C, while Jones took care of the chicken soup and toast. "You suffer more with a simple cold than anyone I've ever seen," she told him on the third day, when he was still languishing in bed. "I hope you never really get sick."

"I don't get colds," he groused. "And I'm not suffering."

"Right," she shot back flippantly. "If you had stayed away from me . . ."

"Hmph," he retorted, blowing his nose.

In between visits to Marc, Cathlyn kept up her regular patient load and spent as much time as she could collating raw data to supply as her portion of a research project on the role of pets in curing depression in elderly people. As he began to feel better, Marc immersed himself in designing plans for the shopping mall. With their time sharply limited, Cathlyn found herself longing for the lazy days they'd spent together when both their lives had been less demanding. To add to her problems, Buffie called to remind her of her promise to give a talk on Angel House before the Junior League. She had hoped Marc would have time to help her put together the presentation, but the best he could do was to find her a moonlighting newspaper photographer to prepare the slide show.

Cathlyn's talk went so well that during the next few weeks Buffie called her repeatedly with pleas for help in doing publicity for the auction.

"If you weren't so damned effective, she'd quit calling," Marc told Cathlyn one afternoon when they had stolen a few hours to take a ride in the country and look at the trees, which had come alive with the reds and golds of autumn.

"But I want the auction to be a success," Cathlyn protested. "The girls are so excited about it, and Jean and Tommy are absolutely overwhelmed. I don't even want to think about their disappointment if this flops."

"It won't flop," Marc assured her, slipping a protective arm around her shoulder. "Remember, I told you, Buff knows all the right people."

"You can say that again," Cathlyn agreed. After all the teas and coffees and planning meetings she'd attended, she sometimes felt she had met every one of them. To her surprise Cathlyn found that she liked many of Buffie's friends. She'd been impressed by the way they'd thrown themselves full-force into preparations for the auction. When the women questioned her about Angel House, she detected a genuine concern for the girls, and heartfelt support for what Jean and Tommy were trying to do.

That was one hurdle she'd cleared more easily than she had anticipated. She never would be part of that life the way Buffie was, but at least she could accept it. She hoped Marc didn't expect any more of her than that. She wondered whether his mother would be as flexible. Cathlyn was anxious to meet Marc's parents. They had spent the early fall touring Europe but, at Buffie's urging, had agreed to come back in time for the auction. The art auction was going to be a big night in more ways than one.

The Saturday morning before the auction,

Jean showed up at Cathlyn's door, as she'd done intermittently over the preceding months when she decided it was time to have a talk. She was overflowing with the excitement of the auction.

"When you first told me about it, I thought you were dreaming," Jean said, opening the familiar white bag from the bakery and sliding out two almond croissants. "Now there's a constant parade of people through the house, and the girls are all fired up about a new rec room. I wonder if I'm the one dreaming."

"It's no dream," Cathlyn assured her. "If it were, I wouldn't have been spending every night for weeks working on it."

"Kind of interfering with your social life, huh?" Jean inquired.

"I've hardly seen Marc." Cathlyn sighed. "He's up against the deadline for the shopping center proposal, and I've been so involved in the auction."

"Have the two of you considered a more permanent arrangement?"

Cathlyn gave her a penetrating look. "You mean, getting married?"

"Well . . ." Jean tossed her head. "Or whatever people do nowadays."

"That's still how they do it," Cathlyn answered. "We haven't actually talked about it. The conversation has wandered in that direction a couple of times, but I don't know whether I'm ready. I'm just not sure."

"The North Shore social scene's getting to you, I can see it," Jean declared, taking a big bite of her croissant. "And I don't blame you. If I get one more sincere, forthright woman with her couture clothes and impeccable makeup, her hands full of wallpaper samples knocking on my door, I don't know what I'm going to do. They always catch me in my furry slippers and rubber gloves, getting ready to scrub the kitchen floor."

Cathlyn laughed. "They want to help. You're their project."

"Yeah," Jean acknowledged. "I spent twenty minutes yesterday explaining to one why yellow silk wallpaper wasn't the answer in a bathroom where a dozen girls were going to be taking showers." Jean paused thoughtfully, watching Cathlyn. "Are you sure you're going to fit in with that crowd?" she asked.

"I'm not sure of anything," Cathlyn admitted. She put another lump of sugar in her coffee and stirred it idly. "But I've been surprised at how much compassion those women have for Angel House. I went into this not expecting to like any of them, but I do."

"So do I," Jean agreed. "I joke about it, but without them we couldn't exist. Their contribution isn't less important; it's just different. And they work damn hard at it."

"I'm beginning to realize that." Cathlyn looked up at her friend. "My mother used to get involved in charitable projects, and I always thought it was a farce. I thought if she really cared, she'd pitch in and get her hands dirty. Now I'm not so sure. I'm beginning to think there's no one right way to do anything."

"Maybe you've developed some perspective," Jean suggested.

Cathlyn nodded. "That's what I spend all day trying to help other people do."

"It's always easier when it's someone else's problems," Jean said, sympathizing. "And I can see your dilemma. Marc's really neat, but . . ." She was silent for a few moments, then she asked bluntly, "Do you love him, Cathlyn?"

A warm smile lighted Cathlyn's face as she thought about Jean's question.

"Never mind, you don't have to answer that," Jean said. "It's written all over your face. And that's the bottom line," she added seriously. "If you really love him, you have to trust him, and somehow you'll work things out."

"I guess so," Cathlyn answered slowly. But she wasn't entirely convinced.

Chapter Nine

THE DAY OF the art auction, Cathlyn was in her office feeding patient information into the computer when Shirley stuck her head through the open door.

"You've got a phone call," she announced. "Didn't you see the light flashing?"

"I guess not," Cathlyn replied absently. "Could I call them back tomorrow?"

"It's one of those girls from Angel House. She says it's a crisis."

"I don't have time for a crisis today." Cathlyn sighed, reaching for the phone.

"It's me, Lisa," said a tremulous voice on the other end of the wire. "I've got a big problem."

"Are you all right?" she asked Lisa, her voice full of concern. "Where are you?"

"I'm okay. I'm in this bar . . ."

"You're in a bar?" Cathlyn sat straight up in her chair. "You can't be, you're only fifteen years old."

"This kid at school told me about his brother saying you could get a free piano if you came to this address," Lisa explained, "and I thought it would be really cool to surprise everybody with a piano for the new rec room."

"A piano?" Cathlyn repeated.

"It's this really neat piano," Lisa said, hurrying on, "and the owner says I can have it, but I need an adult's permission. I can't call Jean because then it wouldn't be a surprise, so I called you."

"Wonderful," Cathlyn remarked. "And just exactly how do you intend to get this 'really neat piano' to Angel House?"

"Well . . ."

There was silence. Cathlyn didn't say anything.

"Actually it's no problem," Lisa continued confidently. "It's on casters. Can we have it?"

Cathlyn didn't follow that reasoning. "Lisa," she said, hedging, "I know you'd really like to have a piano. Maybe we can make some inquiries and try to locate something."

"Oh, Cathlyn, please come," Lisa implored.

"There'll never be another piano like this one!" Her voice rang with excitement.

"Come there?" Cathlyn asked. "You mean, right now?"

"The owner says it has to be right now. Otherwise he'll have it hauled away. Please, Cathlyn!"

Cathlyn looked at the clock. The whole scheme was ridiculous. But it was obviously very important to Lisa. She weighed the situation. If she hurried, she could probably make it out there and still get home in time to dress for the auction. "All right, Lisa," she said, "give me the exact address. I'll be there as soon as I can."

Cathlyn hung up the phone and immediately dialed Marc. Maybe he could think of some fast, cheap, easy way to transport a piano—a big old upright, no doubt. That way she could get the whole thing settled at once. But Marc wasn't in his office. Disappointed, Cathlyn left a message. She'd have to stall the owner until Monday and see whether they could figure something out.

"Shirley," she called to the outer office.

"What do you need, Dr. Tate?" Shirley asked, appearing at the door.

"I have to run an errand . . . it's a long story. But I won't be back for the rest of the afternoon."

"You're never going to get those files on the computer," Shirley scolded as Cathlyn flipped off the power switch. "And I thought you were going to try to leave early to get ready for the art auction. If I know you and your errands, this is going to push you right up against another deadline—"

"I know that," Cathlyn interrupted, buttoning her gray winter coat and wrapping a red angora scarf around her neck. "But I've got a pressing date with a kid and a piano." She looked down at her new black leather pumps and then at Shirley's feet, which were clad in a pair of hot pink jogging shoes. "How are your bunions?" Cathlyn inquired suddenly.

"My bunions?" Shirley followed Cathlyn's gaze to the shoes. "They're much better since I started wearing these shoes. Just like the doctor said."

"Don't you keep another pair of shoes in the office, some that you could wear for a little while?"

"Yes . . . what are you getting at?" Shirley asked suspiciously.

"I need to borrow your shoes for a while, the ones on your feet."

"My jogging shoes?" Shirley stared at her.

"Just for this afternoon," Cathlyn continued persuasively.

"Well, I don't know," Shirley said, bending down to untie her shoes.

"I really appreciate this," Cathlyn told her, quickly shoving her feet into the pink shoes and pulling up the laces.

She was on her way out the door when she had a sudden thought. "One more thing." She turned toward Shirley, who was still standing dumbfounded in the middle of the office holding Cathlyn's high-heeled pumps. "If Marc calls, tell him to come to this address and help me deal with a piano." She stuffed the paper with the address into Shirley's free hand. "It's a bar," she called back as she hurried out the door.

Cathlyn drove slowly past the boarded-up buildings and storefronts with iron bars guarding the windows. "Of all the dumb things to be doing," she muttered as she approached the address Lisa had given her. She pulled up directly in front of the place, wincing as her tires crunched over glass fragments from a broken-out streetlight. She stepped out of the car, took a good look around, and checked again to make sure the car doors were securely locked.

The gusty November wind swirled dirt and scraps of paper and then dropped them along the littered street. She thought about the elegant hotel where she'd be with Marc in just a few hours, sipping white wine and exchanging pleasantries with the rich and the powerful. She suddenly understood how she was different from the women she'd worked with on the auction during the last few weeks. Her life spanned two very different worlds; theirs were caught up in only one. Cathlyn kicked at a wadded-up paper bag, and an empty wine bottle inside clanked against the sidewalk.

Shaking her head, she walked briskly past a window coated with black soot and tugged firmly on the door to the bar. "Lisa," she called out, pulling harder at the door. When it didn't budge, she looked at it more carefully and saw the scrap of cardboard stuck in the corner with the word *closed* scrawled across it. "Lisa, answer me," she shouted, beginning to worry. What if something had happened to her?

Cathlyn was beating hard on the locked door when it opened suddenly and Lisa threw her arms around Cathlyn. "I'm so glad you're here," the girl exclaimed.

"Didja bring the truck?" a gruff voice demanded. Cathlyn looked over Lisa's shoulder at a burly man wearing a stained bartender's apron over his jeans and T-shirt.

"Truck?" Cathlyn questioned, taking an involuntary step back. "Where would I get a truck?"

"That's your problem, lady," the man barked. "I just want to get rid of the piano."

"I told him I was calling a friend who would help me," Lisa interjected hastily. "Come on and look at the piano. You're absolutely going to love it."

"I'll bet," Cathlyn replied. She let Lisa lead her through a maze of cartons, tables, and stacked chairs to the rear of the dingy establishment. The place was musty and dark, and the smell of stale beer and sweat made her want to gag. The man in the apron followed them. He made Cathlyn nervous. This was certainly no place for a fifteen-year-old girl, she decided.

"There it is," said the man, snapping on an eerie yellow spotlight.

"My God!" Cathlyn gasped, staring at the piano. "It's purple."

"Isn't it magnificent?" Lisa purred, stroking the yellowed keys.

"But it's bright purple," Cathlyn repeated. She took a small step closer, unable to take her eyes off the monstrosity. She wasn't sure she'd ever seen anything quite so ugly.

"You're gettin' a real deal." The man stepped closer and patted the piano fondly. "If it weren't goin' to them orphans, I'd charge you a bundle. 'Course, you might wanna paint over them pictures on the sides."

"Pictures?" Cathlyn walked around the piano until she saw the nearly life-size nudes some aspiring artist had probably traded for a few shots of gin.

"Lisa," Cathlyn began firmly, deciding it was time to take the situation in hand.

"Don't worry, I wasn't going to leave them there," Lisa assured her quickly. "You know how good Ellie is at art. I'll have her paint some clothes on them right away."

"Good upright like this would cost you." The man snorted. "If I didn't have to get it out of here tonight, I could sell it for five or six hundred bucks."

"Please!" Lisa begged.

"Wait a minute." Cathlyn tried to remain calm. "You mean, this piano has to be moved tonight? Couldn't it wait until Monday?"

"Nope," the man answered. "I'm movin' out of this dump. Can't take it with me." He turned on his heel. "You got five minutes."

Cathlyn turned to Lisa. "This is out of the question," she said firmly. "We have no way to move a piano today."

"Please, Cathlyn," Lisa pleaded. "Couldn't we just move it out on the street and then figure out something? We'll never get another deal like this."

"That's for sure," Cathlyn said dryly. She fervently wished she had been able to reach Marc before she left the office. Maybe he could have thought of something. Lisa sat down at the old piano, moving her fingers nimbly up and down the keys in a series of arpeggios. Then she slipped into a slow, haunting melody that Cathlyn only vaguely recognized. As Lisa became more and more engrossed, her music built in a series of crescendos so dramatic that even the man in the greasy apron came back to listen.

When the sounds faded to silence, Lisa looked up, her eyes sparkling. "Please, Cathlyn?" she asked softly.

Defeated, Cathlyn shook her head. She wasn't sure what they were going to do, but she supposed they had to try something. "Well, don't just sit there," she finally told Lisa. "Get on the other side and push."

"All right!" Lisa exclaimed, leaping to her feet.

With maximum effort Cathlyn and Lisa managed to maneuver the cumbersome piano through the bar, while the man in the apron shoved tables and boxes out of their path. As soon as they reached the sidewalk, Cathlyn heard the door close and lock behind them. She realized they were on their own.

"Now what?" Lisa asked, leaning against the piano and panting with exertion. "I really hoped you'd bring a truck or something."

"We're going to try the 'or-something' approach," Cathlyn declared. "It's only a few blocks. Go back to the other side and push." Using every ounce of strength, she and Lisa got the piano moving. Once it was under way, the going got easier, except when one of the metal casters stuck in a crack in the uneven sidewalk and the bulky piano lurched dangerously to one side.

They rolled along at a steady pace, attracting very little attention in the scuzzy neighborhood where nothing was unexpected. One old woman, hunched over against the chilly November wind, shook her head in disbelief as she hobbled by, but others passed, swerving out of their way without really looking at them.

"We sure could use some help," Lisa said, huffing, as they steered the piano around a steel grate in the sidewalk. "I wish somebody would offer."

"Don't count on it," Cathlyn replied cynically. "It's called the anonymity of the city. They don't even see us."

"It's not going to be easy to get this thing across the street," Lisa pointed out when the piano came to rest at the edge of a curb.

"That's an understatement," Cathlyn replied, pausing to catch her breath. "Let's shove your end off first." Carefully they eased the purple piano forward until it balanced precariously, as if it were hanging off the edge of a steep cliff. Cars whizzed down the street in front of them.

"Now you hold it exactly like that while I stop the traffic," Cathlyn directed. Quickly she headed for the middle of the intersection, dodging skillfully between moving cars. The bitter wind swirled the car exhaust into her face.

Coughing, she raised her arms and waved them wildly over her head. Miraculously, traffic slowed and crept to a stop. "All right, Lisa, bring her out," Cathlyn shouted, suddenly feeling powerful.

Lisa bumped the purple piano off the curb and struggled to keep it moving across the rough asphalt. When she faltered on the way up, on a slope in the center of the street, Cathlyn rushed over to help her. Together they gave a mighty shove, and the piano mounted the slope. But at the top it lurched dangerously, first left and then right.

"I can't hold on to it," Cathlyn shouted to Lisa as she lost her grip on the corners of the purple piano. She grabbed for the piano leg, but it was too late. The piano made a sharp right turn and started rolling down the incline.

"No!" Cathlyn screamed. She lunged after the runaway purple piano. A cacophony of car horns blasted at her.

"Get that piano," Cathlyn yelled to anyone who might hear. Traffic was at a dead stop in all directions. Horns blared. Drivers stuck their heads out car windows, craning their necks to locate the problem. It wasn't hard to find. The only things moving in the intersection were Cathlyn and Lisa and the purple piano.

"Hey, lady, you better stop that piano before it hits something," yelled a big man in a Honda.

"I'm doing my best," Cathlyn shouted, dashing past him.

"Cathlyn, do something," Lisa screamed.

"Try to catch it from your side," Cathlyn yelled back to her.

Lisa took off, zigzagging between cars that were taking off in all directions, trying to get out of the path of the piano, which was rapidly picking up speed. Cathlyn closed in from the other side. Out of the corner of her eye she saw a squad car pull up a side street, its red lights flashing. A policeman got out, scratching his head as he stared at the traffic snarl.

"Get out of the way," Lisa screamed to the policeman, who only looked around in confusion.

"Move!" echoed Cathlyn. She ran faster, her eyes riveted on the purple piano, careening wildly down the street. It was on a direct collision course with the squad car. Horns honked wildly, and drivers shouted out their windows.

The inevitable was about to happen. The piano was still rolling, and the squad car was dead ahead. Cathlyn couldn't stop it, and she couldn't bear to watch. She scrunched her eyes shut just before the resounding crash. From the sound she knew, even without looking, that the piano had scored a dead-center hit.

Cathlyn stood for a long moment, desperately trying to collect herself. Then she opened her eyes and stood perfectly still, slowly shaking her head. The side of the blue-and-white squad car was bashed in. Wedged up against it, apparently undamaged, was the garish purple piano. Cathlyn had absolutely no idea what to do next. Finally she shoved her hands in her coat pockets, took a deep breath, and walked slowly over to the portly policeman.

He zeroed in on her immediately. "Is this your piano, lady?" he demanded. His face was beefy red.

Cathlyn looked directly into the policeman's angry eyes and smiled. "Yes, Officer, I'm afraid it is."

He looked like he was going to explode. "What the hell is it doing here?"

"Well, sir," Cathlyn began respectfully, "we were moving it and . . ."

"Moving it?" he echoed, looking around. "Where's the truck?"

"That was the problem," Cathlyn explained. "We don't have one."

"If you're moving a piano, you must have a truck," the officer insisted loudly. Horns kept honking, and drivers were gaping at the piano and shouting obscenities at each other.

"But we don't have a truck," Cathlyn shouted over the noise.

The policeman looked at her incredulously. "You stand right there, lady. Don't move. We're going to get to the bottom of this in just a minute." Climbing into his squad car through the back door, because the front door was pinned shut by the piano, he picked up the radio microphone. Cathlyn couldn't quite hear what he said until he raised his voice. "I'm trying to tell you, Joe. It's not a purple car. It's this broad with a purple piano. No, I ain't been over to Murphy's. I'm telling you—just send the backup. And a wagon. No, she don't look dangerous. Never mind, just send them."

"Now, lady," the policeman said, getting out of

the squad car. "Let's try this one more time. You're telling me you're moving this piano, without any truck, and you sent it barreling down the street in all this traffic and smashed it into my squad car. And you did this all by yourself?"

"No," Lisa said, speaking up timidly. "I helped her."

"Shh," Cathlyn warned her.

"Then you can come down to the station too," the policeman roared. "I oughta put the cuffs on you both before you do any more damage."

"Does there seem to be a problem here?" Cathlyn heard Marc's reassuring voice behind her and felt his arm move protectively around her shoulder. She could hardly believe it. He must have come as soon as he'd gotten her message.

"Is this your piano, too, buddy?" the policeman demanded gruffly.

Marc took a long look at the purple piano, his eyes slowly taking in the picture of the exotic nude on the exposed end. "It's one of the most prized possessions in my life," he answered solemnly. The corners of his mouth twitched with hidden laughter.

"What's your name, buddy?" the officer demanded, glowering at Marc.

"Marc Harrison."

"All right, Harrison, you can come down to the station with the rest of them. They're going to throw the book at you," the policeman threatened. Cathlyn winced. Now they were all in trouble. She looked sideways at Marc. If anyone could think of a way out of this mess, he could.

Cathlyn felt someone pushing against her

shoulder and looked around as a young man thrust a microphone in front of Marc. "Excuse me, sir, what did you say your name was?" Behind him, a television cameraman was grinding away.

"Wow!" said Lisa, sidling up to Cathlyn. "That's the evening news."

"They probably picked it up off the police radio." Cathlyn groaned. "Don't you dare say a word," she hissed at Lisa. Lisa nodded mutely, her eyes like saucers as she watched the cameraman shooting footage of everything in sight with the big portable camera braced on his shoulder.

Marc looked at the reporter, at the policeman, then back to the reporter. "You got here just in time," he said smoothly. "You are just about to witness one of Chicago's finest doing a good deed for some orphaned children."

"Huh?" said the policeman.

"This piano was on its way to Angel House, which is a home for girls who have nowhere else to go, when this er . . . um . . . unfortunate accident occurred," Marc went on. The policeman, Cathlyn, and Lisa all stared at him openmouthed. The camera ground on. "And, um . . ." Marc leaned over to read the policeman's name plate. "Sergeant O'Connor here has been able to find it in his heart not only to overlook the accident, which was completely beyond anyone's control, but to help haul the piano for the benefit of these homeless girls." Marc clapped the policeman on the shoulder.

"Is that right, Sergeant O'Connor?" the reporter asked. A paddy wagon pulled up right on cue.

"Well, I er, I . . ." the policeman began.

The cameraman panned to a shot of the squad car. "Well, folks," the reporter was summing up, "we've seen a drama here today that shows us how compassionate our men in blue can be. I guess almost anything can have a happy ending."

The television crew left after a final shot of four hefty policemen hoisting the piano into the back of the paddy wagon. Most of the traffic had cleared out, except for a few onlookers, attracted as much by the TV camera as by the purple piano.

Cathlyn threw her arms around Marc. "You were magnificent," she whispered gratefully.

"How did you ever get yourself into this mess?" he asked, hugging her tight. "When I called your office, Shirley told me she had a feeling I'd better get here right away."

"I . . . well . . . it's a long story." Cathlyn sighed and looked at her watch. "Marc, we've got to hurry. We're going to be late to the art auction."

"I'm hurrying. I didn't know we were going to spend the afternoon ramming pianos into police cars." The dimples in his cheeks were very deep.

Lisa rode in the paddy wagon with the piano, and Marc and Cathlyn followed in his car, where she poured out the whole story of the piano, occasionally managing a weak smile when he convulsed with laughter.

"You've got a heart as big as the Grand Canyon," he told her, squeezing her hand. "Maybe that's part of why I love you so much."

"What do you mean?" Cathlyn asked in confusion. She'd expected him to be angry, or at least irritated, because she'd gotten them all into a dumb situation. And he was telling her how much he loved her?

"You always follow your feelings, Cathlyn, even when it isn't the easy way. And you're never afraid to take a chance." He pulled the car into a parking place in front of Angel House and switched off the engine. "Almost anybody else would have told Lisa no and gone home to get dressed. You didn't. You understood how much the piano meant to her."

"Then you're not angry because we're late?"

Marc put his hands on her cheeks and looked deep into her eyes. "Of course not. I love you just the way you are. I wouldn't change a thing."

Hearing shouts and laughter from Angel House, they quickly got out of the car. Within moments all the girls had congregated on the front porch with Jean, clutching her pink chenille bathrobe, standing right at the front of the group.

"What's going on?" Jean demanded of Cathlyn and Marc, who were approaching the front steps. "Why aren't you at home getting ready for the art auction?" Her voice rose as her eyes traveled beyond them. "And why is there a paddy wagon in front of the house?"

"Lisa has a surprise for you," Cathlyn answered. "If there's a chair on the porch, you'd better sit down."

"It's like nothing you've ever seen," Marc added, slipping his arm around Cathlyn's waist. All eyes turned to the paddy wagon as the policemen opened the rear doors.

"Everybody move," directed Lisa, "we're coming through." With a chorus of excited murmurs the girls drew back, and the policemen heaved the piano out of the wagon and began pushing it up the sidewalk. The color drained from Jean's face.

"That's not really a purple piano with naked ladies on it that those policemen are pushing up my front walk, is it?" she whispered.

"I'm afraid it is," Cathlyn affirmed.

"I'm not even going to ask." Jean shook her head as the parade continued across the porch, into the front hall. Marc thanked the policemen profusely, while Cathlyn and Jean joined the girls in the front hall where the piano reigned in decadent splendor.

"Isn't it fantastic?" Lisa exulted, running her hand fondly over the top of the old upright. The girls gathered around her, giggling at the nude pictures and plinking the piano keys, all chattering at once.

"I assume it's for the rec room?" Jean asked, sounding as though she were still in shock.

"It is," Cathlyn said, patting her friend's arm. "And it's all yours." She looked hurriedly at her watch. "Now, if we don't get moving, we'll never make it to the art auction. See you in an hour or so," she shouted back as she ran down the front walk.

Marc dropped Cathlyn off at her apartment, promising that Jones would pick up her Toyota from in front of the bar. She literally flew from the front door to the shower, unbuttoning her blouse on the way. She still couldn't quite believe what had happened to her, or that Marc had reacted the way he had. The way he'd operated with that policeman had been a stroke of genius. She laughed to herself, remembering Sergeant O'Connor's beefy red face as he stammered in front of the TV cameras. He'd never know what happened to him. She chuckled, stepping into the shower.

But that wasn't what really made the impression, Cathlyn realized as the steaming water washed over her. It was Marc's reaction to her, his support when he could just as easily have told her she'd done a really dumb thing. Maybe they could make this work, she mused. Jean was right. What she had to do was trust him. As long as they were honest with each other, everything could be all right.

A few minutes later Cathlyn stood in front of her bedroom mirror, blow dryer in hand, one eye on the clock. Tossing her slightly damp hair out of her face, she deftly applied her makeup and sprayed her nude body with cologne. Then she slipped into her wispy black lingerie and dropped her black organza gown over her head, carefully sliding her arms into the petaled sleeves. She tugged up the zipper, noting that by any standards the transformation she'd just achieved was remarkable. After giving a final swipe to her flowing hair, Cathlyn picked up her wrap and her purse and sailed out to meet Marc in the lobby.

Chapter Ten

"YOU'RE GORGEOUS," HE SAID, taking her in his arms and kissing her, "and only five minutes late."

"Nothing to it." She smiled up at him demurely. "You did pretty well yourself," she noted. She'd never seen a man look as sexy in a tuxedo as Marc did.

With a grin he appraised her carefully. "I don't think anyone would suspect that you were pushing a purple piano down the street two hours ago, unless, of course, I were to tell them," he said, teasing her.

"You wouldn't!" she exclaimed, her poise momentarily shaken.

"Probably not," he replied, holding the door open for her, "but it would make fascinating conversation."

Marc helped Cathlyn into the waiting limousine, taking her hand as the driver turned up the Outer Drive. A sliver of moon was barely visible over the blackened waters of Lake Michigan, and only a scattering of stars dotted the night sky. Earlier in the evening the air had held a hint of snow, and now a fine white powder dusted the passing cars. The subtle Impressionist music of Debussy was playing softly on the stereo. Marc was sure he had never been more content. He glanced over at Cathlyn, so lovely and poised, and thought about her only a few hours before in those funny jogging shoes, standing nose-to-nose with the burly policeman, arguing over the purple piano. Then he thought about the way she looked in the first light of morning, after they had made love, with her cheeks flushed pink and her hair tumbling around her milky white shoulders. *Marc Harrison,* he thought to himself, *you are one damn lucky man.*

"Happy?" he asked Cathlyn, stroking her hand lightly.

Marc's touch sent a wave of delicious sensation through her. "Oh, yes," she breathed, turning to look at him, "very, very happy."

The limousine pulled around the circular drive in front of the new Continental Hotel, and Marc and Cathlyn stepped out into the cold night air. They walked together through the elegant lobby, up the rich red carpet of the grand staircase to the mezzanine level where the art auction was being held. At the top of the stairs, a television camera was mounted on a tripod and a reporter with a portable microphone was interviewing guests at the auction. Cathlyn shied away, recognizing him as the same reporter who had been on Clark Street earlier.

"Marc," she whispered. "Look! It's him."

"Who?" Marc asked, looking around.

"Excuse me, sir," the reporter said, turning to them. "Are you interested in any particular artist this evening, or are you— Wait a minute!" He looked hard at Marc and Cathlyn. "I've seen you two before. You're the ones with the purple piano."

"Anything for Angel House," Marc said coolly, breezing by the reporter with Cathlyn on his arm. "Just keep walking," he whispered to Cathlyn, guiding her deftly through the crowd that was filtering into the Crown Room. "He doesn't have a portable camera, so he can't follow us tonight."

"Good," Cathlyn said, relieved. "I've had enough of him for one day." As they worked their way slowly though the formally attired crowd, Cathlyn recognized one of the senators from Illinois, the head of a large advertising firm, and a member of the Bears football team and his wife. Several people recognized Marc, who nodded and exchanged polite greetings. But he showed genuine enthusiasm as he clasped the hand of a young man dressed in jeans and sweatshirt, one gold earring, and a pair of thong sandals.

"How are you, Paul?" Marc said warmly.

"Great," the young man answered.

Marc turned to Cathlyn. "This is Paul Marcel," he told her. "I'm sure you've enjoyed his metal sculpture along the lakefront."

Suddenly Cathlyn was awed. She extended her

hand to the world-renowned artist, now totally oblivious to his attire.

"Are you exhibiting tonight?" Marc asked Paul.

"Yes," Paul answered. "Three pieces, all in the center. *The Wings of Gulls* is the best."

"I'll look for it," Marc said, opening the door to the Crown Room for Cathlyn.

Just as Buffie had said, the magnificent room, done in stark contemporary with a silver-and-white decor, was the perfect backdrop for the artwork. Across an expanse of shimmering gray carpet, the paintings were individually displayed on freestanding screens of pure white, softly lit by a myriad of sparkling crystal chandeliers. Small individual spotlights were discreetly placed to highlight the sculpture in the center of the exhibit. The effect was breathtaking.

Near the buffet table, which stretched in an enormous S-curve across one end of the room, people gathered in groups, talking and laughing. Others strolled slowly among the paintings, stopping to admire a particular piece or to talk to the artists, who stood near their work. Cathlyn noticed several people saunter toward the desk where bids for the silent auction were being recorded.

As she scanned the crowd, she saw Jean and Tommy waving to her from across the room. Since Marc appeared to be caught up in a conversation with one of the White Sox owners, Cathlyn eased away and went over to talk to her friends.

"Did you see the six o'clock news?" Jean asked breathlessly as she approached.

Cathlyn shook her head. "Are you kidding? I barely had time to get dressed."

"Too bad"—Jean blinked behind her glasses—"because you were on it."

"I was *what?*" Cathlyn exclaimed.

"You were on the six o'clock news," Tommy chimed in. "You and Marc and"—he chuckled—"that sexy purple piano."

"Oh, no," Cathlyn said with a moan. "You mean, they actually put that on television?"

"Complete with a dissertation on Marc Harrison and his friend. They didn't seem to have your name." Jean grinned. "Your atrocious pink shoes even got on film."

"Oh, no." Cathlyn moaned again. She thought of how ludicrous it all must have looked and fervently hoped everyone else had been too busy getting ready for the auction to have time to watch it.

Just then Buffie Harrison came up behind them and kissed Cathlyn fleetingly on the cheek. "I do hope the piano was worth all the trouble," she said breezily.

"I take it you saw the news too," Cathlyn replied evenly.

"In living color," Buffie assured her. "Perhaps the piano has antique value," she added comfortingly. "Once you get it stripped, you'll be able to evaluate its condition."

"It's pretty easy to evaluate in its present condition," Jean responded dryly.

"Right," agreed Tommy. "An authentic piece

from the early saloon period." Even Cathlyn laughed in response.

"Excuse me," Marc said, joining the group. "I need to steal Cathlyn away. My mother has been anxious to meet her."

"Marc," Cathlyn said as he led her across the room, "are you aware that we—and that stupid piano—were on the six o'clock news?"

"So I've been told." Marc laughed.

"That is not exactly the image I want to portray to your mother—or my patients," Cathlyn protested.

"Why not?" Marc teased. "Isn't that the real you, pink jogging shoes and all?"

Cathlyn rose to the bait. "No, it isn't, and besides, the shoes belong to Shirley. Marc, people are going to think . . ."

Marc stopped in the middle of the crowded room and grinned down at her. "I don't give a damn what anyone thinks," he declared. "I like you just the way you are. And if there weren't so many people around . . ." He caressed the back of her neck with the tip of his finger.

"Marc." Little shivers ran all up and down Cathlyn's back.

"Just wait till I get you home," he promised.

"Marc!" Cathlyn said again. He was still touching her, and she was far more aware of the movement of his single finger under her flowing hair than of all the noise and confusion around them.

"Marc," a genteel voice broke in firmly. "Marc, you promised to bring Cathlyn to meet me, and I've been waiting all evening."

"I'm sorry, Mother." Marc smiled at the elegant gray-haired woman in the mauve chiffon gown. "This is Cathlyn Tate. Cathlyn, my mother, Margaret Harrison."

"I'm happy to meet you, Mrs. Harrison," Cathlyn responded, returning the firm handshake.

"And I am delighted to know you at last." Margaret Harrison's face was warm and expressive, with smile lines etched around her mouth and hazel eyes that looked very much like Marc's. "Buff has told me so much about you, and then tonight, when I saw you on the news and realized how attractive you are, I couldn't imagine why my son has been keeping you from us."

So she'd seen the newscast too. But she didn't seem the least bit taken aback by the wayward piano, Cathlyn realized. In fact, her first reaction seemed to be disappointment that they hadn't met sooner. How odd . . . and how nice.

"Tell me all about your adventure this afternoon, my dear," Mrs. Harrison said, taking Cathlyn's arm and leading her to a small table along one side of the room. "I understand you turned up a real treasure for Angel House."

Cathlyn liked her immediately. She seemed warm and genuine, laughing with delight as Cathlyn recounted the story of the afternoon's escapades.

Marc followed them, watching the two women who meant the most to him as they talked comfortably together. He couldn't very well explain to his mother why he hadn't been able to bring Cathlyn to meet her months ago, before they had left for Europe. She was inordinately proud of being a Harrison and would never understand that he hadn't wanted Cathlyn to know who he was.

He was about to join them at the table when his mother stopped him. "Marc, now that I have finally met this lovely young woman, I'd like a chance to get acquainted. Why don't you go find Andy—he was looking for you earlier—and Cathlyn and I will have a visit."

Marc frowned. He had no interest in Andy when he could be with Cathlyn. But he knew better than to argue with his mother. "All right," he agreed. "And I'll get us all some hors d'oeuvres. Cathlyn and I were rather busy during the dinner hour. We didn't have time to eat." He caressed Cathlyn lightly on her back, hoping that his touch conveyed what he couldn't say. Then he started across the room in search of his brother.

"Hey, Andy," he called, spotting his brother leaving a group near the buffet table. "I understand you're looking for me."

"Boy, am I looking for you," Andrew answered, gripping his brother's shoulder. "Get yourself another glass of wine and come with me."

Wine in hand, Marc followed his brother to a quiet corner of the room behind a marble pillar.

"Old buddy," Andrew began, "you've got yourself one hell of a problem."

"What do you mean?" Marc asked, uneasy at the ominous tone of Andrew's voice. He took a swallow of his wine.

"Remember that magazine interview you did last year for *Chicago Scene?*"

"The Bachelor of the Month," Marc said. "The one they were going to run in the December issue."

"Not were," Andrew said flatly. "Are."

"No, they're not," Marc replied calmly. "I took care of that last summer, remember? I retracted permission for the article."

"You only thought you retracted permission," Andrew said, correcting him. "That was a pretty juicy piece. They apparently got together with their lawyers and decided to go ahead with it, anyhow. They kept it all hush-hush, no advance publicity, so you wouldn't apply any pressure."

"You've got to be kidding." Marc downed the rest of his wine in one swig and stared at his brother.

"Wish I were, but I've spent the better part of the evening with the editor of *Chicago Scene.* The magazine, complete with bare-chested centerfold and a lurid interview, will hit the newsstands next week."

"No, dammit!" Marc pounded his fist on the pillar. "I'll stop it. I'll get a lawyer."

"I am a lawyer," Andy pointed out. "It's too late for lawyers. We could try for an injunction, but we haven't got a chance in a million. The magazines are off the press and on their way."

"Dammit, Andy, there's got to be a way out." Marc looked across the room at Cathlyn, remembering the flippant remarks he'd made to the writer about women. It had been a stupid thing to do in the first place, but now he'd never be able to explain it to Cathlyn.

"The way out was not to make that poker bet in the first place, or at least not to carry through and do the interview," Andrew said. "And on three queens!" he added wryly.

"Shut up," Marc snapped at him. "You're telling me I have to stand back and let a stupid poker game ruin the rest of my life?"

"You're worried about Cathlyn, aren't you?" Andy said.

"That story is going to hang me out there as the very person I've spent months persuading her I'm not," Marc retorted in a steely voice. "How the hell do I convince her I'm not just a rich playboy when she's holding a picture of me draped across a bar, naked to the waist, discussing the advantages of round beds?"

"Beats me, fella," Andrew replied. "But you'd better figure out something fast."

"You bet I will," Marc said with a scowl. "Where's that editor?"

"Over there by the buffet table." Andy pointed. "But, Marc"—he put a restraining hand on his brother's arm—"don't do something you'll regret."

"I already have," muttered Marc. He turned and strode off toward the portly editor of *Chicago Scene.*

From her seat at the table opposite Margaret Harrison, Cathlyn had a clear view of a good part of the Crown Room. When she saw Marc striding purposefully toward the buffet table, she assumed he was going to get their hors d'oeuvres. He stopped short of the table, however, and grabbed a middle-aged man by the shoulder, turning him around roughly until they were face-to-face.

What was he trying to do? Cathlyn thought, puzzled. For the next several minutes she only partially heard Margaret Harrison's lengthy description of the Scottish Highlands, trying to nod at appropriate moments. The real focus of her attention was the scene near the buffet table. The two men appeared to be very angry, gesturing wildly with their hands, both talking at once. As their voices grew louder, Cathlyn caught a few words: "magazine . . . December issue . . . centerfold . . . lawyers." Marc looked more angry than she'd ever seen him, and the other man was red in the face, his jowls trembling. The people around them had gathered in a half circle. Cathlyn saw one of them put a hand on the portly man's shoulder, as though trying to calm him, but the man shook it away.

"Whatever my son is discussing with that gentleman is certainly not very pleasant," Mrs. Harrison commented, and Cathlyn was aware that Marc's mother had also abandoned their conversation and turned to watch the confrontation.

"It certainly isn't," Cathlyn agreed. "Perhaps if I join them . . ." She rose from her chair. Just at that moment Marc reached out and grabbed the man's lapel. Simultaneously the middle-aged man swung his fist at Marc. Cathlyn gasped softly. Marc ducked and without hesitation gave the portly man a hard shove that nearly landed him in a tray of canapés.

Cathlyn took off across the room, watching with relief as one of the portly man's companions broke his fall just before he hit the buffet table. "Marc!" she called out.

Marc looked up at her and back at the man, who was trying to steady himself. He then slowly adjusted his dinner jacket.

"Are you all right?" Cathlyn asked, taking his arm.

"I'm fine," he growled, yanking away from her.

"You'll pay, Harrison," the other man snarled.

"So will you," Marc answered in a voice like frozen steel. He turned abruptly and took Cathlyn's hand. "Come on," he said gruffly, "let's get out of here." Cathlyn almost had to run to keep up with him as he strode across the room. She could feel the anger in his hard, tense muscles. She tried to ignore the curious stares and whispered comments as people pulled back, allowing them to pass.

"That was a damn fool thing to do," exploded a distinguished, elderly man with thick eyebrows and a full head of silver-gray hair. "Haven't you grown out of saloon brawls?" Cathlyn felt Marc stiffen and didn't need anyone to tell her she was about to meet his father.

"Now, John—" Mrs. Harrison interceded.

Marc interrupted her. "Father's right," he said. "That wasn't one of my better moves." He shoved his hands into his pockets, and Cathlyn saw him grin for the first time since he'd introduced her to his mother. "But I can't say that I regret it. The man's a real ass." He turned toward Andy, who had joined them. "Go call my car, will you, Andy? I think we've been here long enough." Without comment his brother nodded agreement.

"I assume that this is the woman your mother has been telling me about," Marc's father said, his eyes softening as he looked at Cathlyn.

"Father, this is Cathlyn Tate," Marc replied formally. His jaw was tight.

"I'm glad to see you do show some good judgment," he told his son as he took Cathlyn's hand in both his own. "It's high time we got acquainted."

"I'm sorry we won't be able to join you," Marc said, resting his arm lightly on Cathlyn's shoulder.

"I think it would be all right for you to stay," his mother urged, but Marc shook his head. She turned to Cathlyn. "But you'll both come to dinner soon?"

"Of course," Cathlyn responded graciously. "I'm happy to have met you both." And I certainly wish it could have been under different circumstances, she thought to herself. She wondered what could have made Marc so incredibly angry.

Marc took her arm and guided her quickly through the crowded room, nodding to several people along the way. Cathlyn detected a few sidelong glances but not many. She suspected that with so many people in the room, only those in the immediate vicinity were even aware of what had occurred.

"Marc," Cathlyn began when they were finally

alone in the limousine. "Whatever possessed you to argue with that man?"

"I told you, he's an ass. Beyond that, I'd rather not discuss it."

"If that's the way you want it." Cathlyn drew back, feeling hurt and shut out.

"Cathlyn," he whispered, his voice hoarse. He took her in his arms and kissed her deeply, holding her tight, almost ferociously, as though he were afraid she might disappear. "I love you, Cathlyn," he whispered fiercely into her hair. "My God, I love you."

Cathlyn buried her head in his shoulder. "Yes, Marc," she whispered back, "I know." And yet she also knew there was a part of him that was still separate from her, a distant part she didn't share.

They rode in silence for several minutes, with Marc cradling her in his arms. He was aware of the wall between them but was afraid to break it down. He wished again that he hadn't done the interview. He'd been mad as hell about losing that poker game, and he'd gone ahead with the interview the next day. Like an adolescent responding to a dare, he'd realized afterward. And he'd said a lot of things he shouldn't have, smart-ass remarks he didn't mean.

That had been his first mistake. His second had been taking their word that they wouldn't print the story. He should have known better than to make a gentleman's agreement with someone who didn't know the meaning of the term. The next move was to get another legal opinion. Maybe Andy was wrong, although he rarely was. But it was hard to believe there wasn't some recourse, some way to keep that magazine off the streets.

"I wish you'd tell me what's bothering you," Cathlyn murmured. "Don't you trust me?"

Her words stung Marc. Before he told her, he needed to know where he stood. He'd been right about waiting the first time. She'd as much as admitted she wouldn't have gone out with him if she'd known who he was. Chances were he was right again. He knew what a premium she put on values. Andy seemed to think he had a week. He wouldn't wait that long—just a day or two until he was sure what was going to happen.

"It's nothing important, Cathlyn," he reassured her with a hug. "Just a business problem, a man who broke his word."

"No wonder you're angry," she said sympathetically, glad he'd at least confided that much. "Deception is the one thing I can't handle, either. I guess you know that." Suddenly she sat up straight and looked out the car window. "Where are we going?" she asked, realizing they had passed her street.

Marc looked down at her for a long moment, hoping he'd made the right decision. "I'm taking you home with me," he said softly. "I want to be with you tonight."

Chapter Eleven

MARC WAS ALL that was on her mind when Cathlyn drove to work Monday morning. She barely saw the gray November drizzle, remembering instead their weekend together. She'd gone home with him after the art auction and hadn't returned to her own apartment until Sunday night. It had been a magical time. She thought about awakening with him, bathed in the red glow of the sunrise, sharing their love just as the first fingers of dawn stretched across the lake. Her mood was mellow, as though nothing in the world could ever go wrong.

She pulled into the parking lot earlier than usual and decided to pass through the newsstand down the street. Wandering through the racks, she picked up a copy of *Chicago Scene,* which a boy was just putting out. While she waited at the cash register, she flipped through the magazine, looking for a feature article on Chicago's fifty best restaurants. Maybe she'd take Marc to dinner, she mused.

The magazine fell open to the center, and Cathlyn's face turned white. She stood frozen, unable to comprehend what she saw. Marc was staring back at her from the double-page spread, a rakish grin on his face. His body was totally naked, at least to the point where it disappeared behind the red-padded top of the bar. BACHELOR OF THE MONTH LIKES SKIING, SCOTCH, AND BROADS IN WHITE MINK, screamed the headline.

"Hey, lady, what you got there?" a gruff voice

interrupted. Cathlyn couldn't take her eyes off the picture. "Lady," he tried again. "You gonna pay for those?"

"Oh, yes . . ." Cathlyn replied numbly, handing the other magazines and a twenty-dollar bill to the man at the cash register. She clutched the picture of Marc.

"What else ya got there?" the man inquired, peering over the counter. "Oh, yeah, *Chicago Scene.* He looks like a real stud, don't he?" the man commented, perusing the picture. "I better order some more. Those are gonna sell out quick," he muttered, making a note. Cathlyn turned away.

"Lady, your change," the man called after her.

"Oh, yes," Cathlyn murmured absently, returning to pick up the handful of bills.

"That guy must really turn you on, lady," the man observed as Cathlyn walked away with Marc's picture still grinning up at her from the open magazine.

She walked outside, the bitter wind spraying rain in her face and across the magazines she was holding. She stood there in a daze, the droplets soaking into the pages, pockmarking them with dark water spots. Almost without thinking, Cathlyn turned into the deli. She picked up a white Styrofoam cup of coffee from the counter, dropped a dollar bill in the basket, and settled herself at a small table near the back. Unbuttoning her coat, she began to read.

"Easy money, snazzy cars, and long-legged blondes are major ingredients in Marc Harrison's life," the article began. "This Bachelor of the Month subscribes to a simple philosophy: 'Play today, or you might regret it tomorrow.' "

Cathlyn took a large swallow of coffee, so hot that it scorched her tongue. She read on, forcing her eyes to move word by word down the columns. She studied pictures of Marc in swim trunks with a towel slung over his shoulder, of Marc in a tuxedo, leaning casually against a red Alfa Romeo, of Marc in jeans and a blue sweatshirt, looking thoughtfully out his penthouse window.

"Marc describes himself as a self-made man," the article said, "claiming to have set aside his family trust money (which measures in the millions) to earn his own way as an architect. He contends you don't have to be stuffy to be rich. 'Some people get so caught up in their charities that they miss out on the better things in life,' he says. No one could accuse our bachelor of anything like that," the article continued. "The hot night spots get hotter when he shows up, and the women take note. 'I like broads in white mink the best,' he says. 'They're the sexiest.' He's been known to arrive at parties with one on each arm —usually blond, always beautiful."

Cathlyn drank more coffee. The article went on and on, detailing Marc's escapades, describing him skiing, swimming, sailing, and racing cars. When she came to the end, Cathlyn closed the magazine and stared blankly at the wall in front of her. At first she was numb, almost totally devoid of emotion. She waited for the anger, but it never came. Instead, an overwhelming sadness washed over her.

He had deceived her, the same way her father had deceived her mother. The open, honest relationship she thought they had was nothing but a sham. There must be some explanation, a voice inside her cried. Cathlyn held the coffee cup with both hands, turning it around slowly. No doubt Marc could provide lots of excuses—her father always did. But the fact of the matter was, she'd thought she had something she didn't.

She knew she couldn't go on kidding herself. That gentle, compassionate man she had fallen so deeply in love with was nothing more than a beautiful fantasy. She looked at the magazine in disgust. This was the Marc Harrison she'd been warned about; the man she loved was Marc Harrison, the dream. Mechanically she stood up, leaving the magazine behind her on the table. She'd go now and get it over with. No point in dragging this out any longer. It wasn't going to get easier.

It was still raining when Cathlyn walked up the steps of the brownstone that housed Marc's office; a fine, misty, bone-chilling rain. She raked her boots across the raffia mat and opened the heavy wood-paneled door. Inside, across the royal blue Oriental carpet, the carefully manicured blond secretary looked up from filing her nails. "Yes, may I help you?" she inquired pleasantly.

"I'd like to see Mr. Harrison," Cathlyn replied, her voice deadly calm.

"Do you have an appointment?" the secretary asked. "He only sees people by appointment."

"Please tell him Cathlyn Tate is here," she answered. "I won't disturb him for very long."

The secretary hesitated and then pressed a button. "Yes?" Marc's voice echoed through the intercom.

"A Cathlyn Tate is here. She wants to see you. I explained that she needed to make an appointment . . ."

A door along the side of the reception area opened, and Marc strode out, covering the room in a few steps to gather Cathlyn in his arms. She tensed and pulled back. "It's all right," he whispered softly into her hair. "Charlene won't mind."

She's probably used to it, Cathlyn thought to herself. "May I see you in your office?" she asked Marc in a cool, businesslike voice clearly designed to hold him at a distance.

"Of course," he replied, looking puzzled.

He followed her across the reception room, and once she was inside his private office, he closed the door behind them. "Cathlyn," he began, touching her shoulder. "Is something wrong?"

"Please sit down, Marc," she replied, gesturing toward his desk chair.

He gave her an odd look and, as though sensing she was in charge, followed her direction without comment.

Resting her hands lightly on the front of his desk, she looked him directly in the eye. She couldn't let him touch her, couldn't get near him, or she might not be able to go through with what had to be done. For a few seconds all she did was look at him, allowing herself one brief moment before it was over. He'd meant more to her than anyone else ever had. If only it could have been the way she thought it was.

When she spoke, her voice was cool. "Marc," she said, "I understand now why you got in the fight at the art auction." She watched the color drain from his face.

"You saw the magazine article?" he said, choking. "It wasn't supposed to be out for another week, and I was going to tell you—"

"You are always 'going to tell me,' " she interrupted in a controlled voice. "But it never quite occurs."

"But, Cathlyn—" he protested, rising to his feet.

Cathlyn raised her hand. "No, Marc," she said with quiet authority, "please sit down and let me finish what I have to say." He hesitated and then sank back in his chair.

"I've hoped and dreamed . . . I thought I was so very close to you," she said in carefully measured tones. "But today I finally realized that that's all it's been—hopes and dreams of the way I wanted things to be. Not the way things are."

"Cathlyn—" he began.

"I'm not finished," she said firmly. "I don't want to see you again, Marc. No more lies. No more deception. You knew right from the beginning that was the one thing I can't handle."

He looked stricken, but she plunged ahead. "I don't want to see you. I don't want to talk to you. I don't want to have any contact with you whatsoever."

"Cathlyn, stop—" he roared, coming to his feet.

Cathlyn continued in the same chilling voice. "You have already done enough to hurt me." She took a deep breath. "I loved you, Marc—"

Her voice breaking, she turned abruptly on her heel and ran out of the office, across the reception room, and out onto the sidewalk where she broke into a run, dodging through crowds of pedestrians and leaving a string of honking cars behind her as she raced across the street. She ran and ran, her boot heels clicking against the wet concrete, until she couldn't run any more. Finally she slowed to a walk, her muscles shaking from exertion, her breath coming in hard gasps. Glancing quickly over her shoulder, she found that she was alone, surrounded by the nameless, faceless city.

She walked aimlessly but steadily, the light rain misting her face and settling in her hair until the curls hung in limp strands. When she came to Michigan Avenue, she turned north along the lake, which was churning with white-caps beneath the gray November sky. She leaned into the wind that bit at her face, cracking her lips and chilling her ears until they were so cold, she had to cover them with her gloved hands. Unthinking and uncaring, she was totally alone, without even the cries of the birds to pierce the desolate howling of the wind.

Still she walked, the blocks stretching behind her, until she came to the street that turned off toward her apartment building. She was almost past the corner when she recognized it. She and

Marc had walked there together so often. His image haunted her and she tried desperately to push it aside. With every step she was running away. She knew it, but she couldn't help it. She couldn't go back and face him. She loved him too much.

Just keep walking, she told herself. One foot and then the other, walking and walking. But she continued to think about him. Would she ever erase the memory of his face when she told him she wouldn't see him again? Or would it one day blend into another memory—that disgusting centerfold that would grin at her for the rest of her life? It would be so easy to pretend it hadn't happened, to close her eyes and go on the way they were. That must have been what her mother had decided to do. Since she was a little girl Cathlyn had vowed it wouldn't be like that for her.

When she reached the door of her apartment, Cathlyn was so cold, she could barely hold the key steady enough to fit it in the lock. The phone was ringing when she opened the door. It was still ringing when she took off her coat, hung it up, and walked into the kitchen to put on water for tea. Finally it stopped for a minute or so, but then it began again. Cathlyn knew she couldn't stand the incessant ringing for long, but she wasn't about to pick up the receiver. There was no one in the world she wanted to talk to. Before the phone was silent again, the water had boiled and Cathlyn had poured it into the teapot to steep. The answering machine, Cathlyn thought suddenly—that was the solution. For only the second or third time since she'd bought it, she flipped it on. She hated answering machines. You were either home or you weren't, and if you weren't, the person could call back. But at least it would silence the phone.

Chilled so thoroughly that even the tea couldn't warm her, Cathlyn went into the bathroom to draw a tub of hot water. She waited until it was almost full before she refilled her teacup and climbed out of her cold, damp clothes. Her legs were red and chapped where the wind had blown under her skirt. Her cheeks were almost raw. The tender skin stung as she slipped down into hot water to her chin. She tried to relax in the soothing heat of the water, but she hurt, outside and in. She looked at the bottle of bubble bath perched on the side of the tub. She'd be using it alone now.

"Damn!" she said aloud. Was he going to be everywhere she turned? Part of her every thought? Sadly she shook her head, knowing the answer was yes, at least for a while. He'd been part of everything she'd done for so long, part of all her hopes and dreams and plans. In one clean stroke she had cut him out of her life—but out of her thoughts and dreams? It wouldn't be that easy.

Late in the afternoon her doorbell rang. She didn't even go to the peephole to see who it was. It didn't matter. The bell rang again and again, punctuated by heavy pounding on the door. Cathlyn pulled her bathrobe tight around her and took another sip of her tea. After almost fifteen minutes the apartment was silent again.

When Cathlyn turned out the lights on her way to bed, she noticed the red light on the telephone answering machine blinking furiously. Maybe she'd play back the messages, she decided, just to see who had called. She flipped the button, and Marc's voice filled the apartment, frightening her with its intensity.

"For God's sake, Cathlyn," he commanded, "turn off this blasted machine and at least let me know you're all right. Call me at home immediately."

Then came Shirley. "Dr. Tate, I've been calling you all day. Where have you been? Obviously you're at home because you've turned on your machine," she rattled on. "I was ready to notify the police when I called Marc and he told me what had happened. Then I didn't know what to do because—" Cathlyn punched the fast-forward button, turning Shirley's voice into an indistinguishable high squeal.

After Shirley, a salesman began a pitch for some sort of real-estate deal. Cathlyn hit fast forward again. Then she heard Jean's voice. "You turkey! You know how I hate these machines. And speaking of turkeys, I'm calling to invite you to come for Thanksgiving." She paused. "With or without Marc. I just phoned Shirley. She's beside herself. Call me when you're ready to talk. I'll bring the croissants." There was a moment of silence, then another click as Jean apparently called back. "One more thing," she said. "If you don't want to talk at all, just come for Thanksgiving. I won't bring it up." Cathlyn smiled. Jean was a good friend.

Marc's voice came back on the speaker, and Cathlyn shivered inside. "Why don't you answer your door? Dammit, Cathlyn, I know you're in there. Are you all right?"

Should she call him? No, she decided, absolutely not.

Cathlyn was on her way to bed when the pounding on the door began again. Three hard raps. Silence. Three more. "This is the police," a gruff voice announced through the bolted door. "Open up or we're coming in."

The police? Cathlyn panicked. What could the police want? "Just a minute," she called back in a shaky voice. Still in her robe, she unbolted the door but left the heavy chain in place. Opening the door a crack, she peeked out. Two uniformed policemen stood outside, guns drawn. "Yes?" she said, still frightened.

"Police," they said again, holding up identification badges in small leather wallets. "Are you Cathlyn Tate?"

"Yes, I am Cathlyn Tate," she replied in a more confident voice.

The two policemen looked at each other and put their guns back in the holsters. "What are you doing here, ma'am?" the younger one asked.

"I live here," Cathlyn answered patiently.

"Yeah, but, lady, you were reported missing," the policeman protested. "There's an all-points out on you."

"What?" Cathlyn asked.

"There's an all-points bulletin out. They're looking for you all over town," the other policeman confirmed. "You're sure you're Cathlyn Tate?" he asked suspiciously.

"I'm absolutely certain," Cathlyn assured him.

"So where have you been?"

"I went for a walk, and then I came home and took a bath. I've been here ever since." Cathlyn was beginning to be annoyed. "Is there something wrong with that?"

"No, lady, guess not," the policeman answered, shaking his head. "Sorry to have disturbed you."

"Wait just a minute," Cathlyn called after them. "Exactly who reported me missing?"

"Beats me," the younger officer answered. "You know, Joe?"

"No," the other policeman said thoughtfully, "except the captain was muttering something about some guy named Harrison."

"Thank you very much," Cathlyn said curtly. "That answers my question."

She bolted and double-locked the door before turning toward the bedroom. The red light on the answering machine was flashing again. No doubt the radio news station had picked up the all-points bulletin, and someone who knew her probably had heard it. Cathlyn groaned. She could see Marc wasn't going to make this easy.

Cathlyn called a cab to take her to the office the next morning because her car was already downtown. She had decided to go right ahead with her life and keep everything as normal as possible. It seemed the only logical approach.

"Dr. Tate!" Shirley accosted her as soon as she

opened the office door. "I was so worried about you. Everybody was so worried. I got all these phone calls and I didn't know what to do and I—"

"Good morning, Shirley," Cathlyn said coolly. For a moment she was afraid Shirley was going to hug her.

"Dr. Tate, are you all right?" Shirley demanded.

"I'm just fine, Shirley," Cathlyn said calmly. "Is my list of appointments on my desk?"

"I didn't know if you were coming in, so I didn't know if I should cancel them. Marc has already called twice, and you have to call him right away—"

"Shirley!" Cathlyn interrupted. "I do not wish to speak with Mr. Harrison under any circumstances. Is that clear?" It was hard even to say the words. But she had to stick to it. It had to be a sharp, clean break.

Shirley stared skeptically at Cathlyn. "You can't run away forever, you know," she chided.

Cathlyn ignored the comment. "Please bring my list of appointments as soon as possible," she said, opening the door to her office. "And Shirley," she added, "I would like to know who is on the telephone before I take any calls."

"Yes, Dr. Tate," Shirley replied. "And boy, are you crabby today," Cathlyn heard her mutter as she closed her office door.

"I am not," Cathlyn grumbled to herself. "I just need to get on with things." She opened her blinds and saw nothing but the slate-gray sky and the sleet splattering against the glass. From where she stood, the world looked cold, dismal, and very uninviting. How appropriate, she thought.

With a brisk knock Shirley opened the door and dropped the appointment sheet on her desk. "Mr. Harrison is on the phone again," she announced.

"Shirley, I've already told you, I don't wish to speak to him," Cathlyn said, bristling.

"Just thought I'd give you another chance," Shirley replied glibly. "It's always nice to let people correct their mistakes." Cathlyn glowered at her retreating back.

The day dragged on. Shirley picked up lunch for both of them at the deli without even asking whether Cathlyn wanted any. Cathlyn ate her turkey sandwich without comment. Turkey made her think about Thanksgiving, which was only a week away. Sighing, Cathlyn called her sister to tell her something had come up, and she and Marc would not be able to be there for Thanksgiving, after all. It was a hard phone call to make. For weeks she had been looking forward to having her sister meet him. But now that wouldn't be necessary. That part of her life was over.

Somehow Cathlyn managed to get through the day, and the next day, and the one after that, until finally she had made it through an entire week without Marc. She missed him more than she ever thought it was possible to miss another human being, but gradually the sharp pain diffused into a dull ache that was always with her.

After Thanksgiving the city turned its attention to Christmas. Store windows up and down Michigan Avenue came alive with animated scenes of Santa's Workshop, the sugarplum fairy, and fat, pink cherubs. The gray November sleet changed to snow that piled up in drifts along the curbs. Shoppers bustled along the streets, juggling bulky packages, hurrying excited children past street-corner Santas ringing their bells. The magic of Christmas was everywhere, but Cathlyn did not feel part of it. On her way to work one early December day, she trudged past the Salvation Army band, clad all in blue, scarcely hearing their joyous carols. Would the ache deep inside her ever go away?

And still Marc persisted. He left daily messages with Shirley, which Cathlyn never returned. At home, she kept her answering machine on almost all the time. Otherwise the phone rang incessantly. Sometimes she wavered, staring at the phone, even touching the receiver. Each time she renewed her determination and turned the machine back on.

"Damn," Marc exclaimed one Tuesday evening, slamming the telephone down for the third time since dinner. Every time he called Cathlyn, he got the answering machine. He figured he'd left at least a thousand messages for her. With a dark scowl on his face he paced back and forth across the thick blue carpet in his library.

Somehow he had to make her listen so he could explain what had happened. He stopped pacing and stood gazing out of his window, watching the snow blanket the lights of the city below him. Millions of people out there, he thought to himself, and only one he cared about. He wondered if Cathlyn still cared, if she even listened to the messages he left her. Shirley gave him a daily report on her, how she looked, what she ate for lunch, whether she was working too hard. But that wasn't enough.

Marc walked over to his desk and picked up a picture of Cathlyn he'd taken aboard the *Sea Sprite.* Her hair was blowing in the breeze, her nose was peeling, and her eyes sparkled with happiness. She had turned into a pretty fair sailor, he thought proudly, with a little instruction, of course. By next summer she would probably be able to crew for him. Angrily Marc threw the picture across the desk. Dammit! If Cathlyn had her way, there wasn't going to be a next summer for them—or any future at all, for that matter. He couldn't believe she didn't love him. Not after what they had shared.

"Jones!" he roared. "I need you."

When his valet appeared at the library door, Marc asked him bluntly, "Jones, have you ever been in love?"

The sedate Jones was momentarily taken aback. "Actually, sir," he replied in his proper British accent, "there was a young Irish lass some years ago."

"Why didn't you marry her?" Marc persisted.

"A silly squabble, as I recall, and she took up with someone else." Jones's face clouded at the memory.

Marc banged his fist on the table. "I'll be damned if I'm going to let that happen to me," he declared.

"Are you referring to Miss Tate, sir?"

"I most certainly am. There must be some way to show her how much I love her."

Jones wrinkled his brow. "I assume you have tried all the traditional approaches, sir? Dinner, wine, flowers—that sort of thing?"

"That's a little tricky," Marc answered glumly. "She won't even talk to me."

"Oh, I see," Jones replied. "Perhaps you should try some less traditional approaches," he suggested.

Marc's interest was piqued. "Like what?" he asked.

"I don't really have any specific suggestions, sir. However, I did read once about a gentleman who wooed a young lady with a string quartet playing romantic songs in her courtyard for an evening."

"Really?" Marc's eyes gleamed. "And it worked?"

"It was the wedding announcement that I read, sir."

"By God!" Marc slammed his fist down hard on the desk. "I ought to be able to come up with something better than a string quartet."

Jones's mouth twitched behind his beard. "I'm sure you can, sir," he said. "However, you need to be prepared for the consequences."

"What consequences?" Marc looked up.

"If you are certain your plan will work," Jones said with a benevolent smile, "you had best alert

Tiffany's promptly. I understand there can be quite a shortage of quality diamonds during the holiday season."

"I'll take care of it," Marc replied crisply. "That, and a few other things too."

Chapter Twelve

CATHLYN COULDN'T BELIEVE her eyes. She'd been walking from the parking lot the same way she did every morning, fitting in with the flow of people, not paying much attention to anything, when she sensed that something out of the ordinary was happening. It didn't take long to figure out what it was.

Right in the middle of the plaza, squarely in front of the Hartford Building, stood the most enormous snowman she had ever seen. He was the traditional sort of snowman, complete with a black top hat, red plaid scarf, and lopsided grin. But he was huge, at least twenty feet tall. She crossed the snow-covered street and joined the laughing, chattering crowd for a closer look.

A snowman like that was every kid's dream, Cathlyn thought, standing on tiptoe to see past the people in front of her. Now that she was closer, he seemed to dominate everything else. Balanced on one of his stick arms, which must have been an entire tree limb rather than a stick, was something that looked like a rectangular slab of ice. Cathlyn craned her neck to get a better look. That wasn't ice—it was a large piece of clear acrylic with something printed on it.

She couldn't quite read the words, but evidently people who were closer could, because there was much spontaneous laughter and conversation going on. It must be some sort of advertisement, Cathlyn decided, turning away. It certainly did attract attention. Then she heard her name and turned around to see who was calling to her.

"I wonder who Cathlyn is?" a young woman asked her red-cheeked companion.

"I don't know," came the giggling reply. "I'd like to know who Marc is."

Quickly Cathlyn elbowed her way to the front of the crowd where she could read the sign. Slowly she mouthed the bright blue words, trying to digest them: "Please come back, Cathlyn. I'm cold without you. Love, Marc."

Cathlyn's eyes opened wide in absolute disbelief. How could Marc do this to her? And right here in front of her office where the whole world could see it! Within the hour everyone on Michigan Avenue was going to know about the snowman. By noon, half the city would be talking about it. And Cathlyn wasn't exactly a common name.

She stared incredulously at the huge snowman towering over her. How did Marc do it? It would have taken a forklift to raise those huge snowballs on top of each other. He must have hired a crew to work half the night. The buttons looked like bowling balls. For that matter, so did the mouth and the eyes. And the scarf . . . on closer inspection it wasn't a scarf at all but probably fifteen or twenty yards of red plaid wool. And where had Marc ever found that enormous black top hat?

Slowly Cathlyn backed through the crowd, unable to take her eyes from the giant snowman. She didn't know whether to laugh or cry as she turned and walked briskly into the building, darting into the seclusion of an empty elevator. She spent the next few moments composing herself before stepping out on the twenty-seventh floor. Head held high, shoulders back, she walked purposefully into her office.

"Good morning, Shirley," she called out.

Shirley emerged from behind a large, red poinsettia, grinning broadly at Cathlyn. "Good morning," she responded with a meaningful raise of her eyebrow.

Cathlyn looked directly into Shirley's eyes. "Yes," she said, "I saw the snowman."

"It would be difficult to miss," Shirley commented, stifling a giggle.

"And," Cathlyn added firmly, "I have chosen to ignore it." She unbuttoned her coat and disappeared into her office.

Shirley poked her head in the door. "Ignoring that snowman is going to take persistence. It will probably be out in the plaza until the spring thaw."

"Don't remind me," Cathlyn said with a grimace. "Just hold my calls so I don't have to discuss it with two hundred and twenty-four of my nearest and dearest friends."

"Suit yourself," Shirley said. "But it would be smarter and simpler to make up with Marc."

"Go away." Cathlyn glowered. She wished it were that simple. But it wasn't.

Despite her order to hold all phone calls, Cathlyn was forced to discuss the snowman with every patient she saw. Mrs. Bixby went on at great length, chattering about how romantic it all was. Tears filled her eyes as she described how Mr. Bixby had stamped out "I love you" in the snow in front of the one-room schoolhouse where she had taught more than fifty years before.

"You never forget things like that," she said nostalgically. "A man who is that imaginative is one you'll be happy with the rest of your life. You take some advice from me, young lady," she said, shaking a gnarled finger at Cathlyn. "You marry that man. Don't you let him get away."

"I'll think about it." Cathlyn sighed. How could she not think about it? Everyone she talked to gave her a version of the same advice.

They just don't understand, Cathlyn thought, opening the morning paper the next day. Idly she thumbed through the pages, bypassing the grisly story of a Middle Eastern terrorist group in search of something lighter. She found it. Right in the center of the local news section was a large color picture of the snowman grinning back at her. The brilliant blue words on the sign screamed like a neon light.

"Oh, no." Cathlyn groaned. She should have

known. It made a perfect human-interest story to highlight the first big snowfall of winter.

The second day of the snowman's life wasn't much better for Cathlyn than the first. Shirley informed her that the picture had gone out over the wires, and people from New York to California now knew Marc was cold without Cathlyn. Apparently it didn't make the Detroit paper, she thought with relief, because so far her sister hadn't called.

By the end of the week, most of the gossip had subsided, and Cathlyn was almost used to the funny fellow greeting her every day when she came to work. But every morning she found herself reading the sign again, and every morning she felt the same pang of loneliness. On Friday she almost called Marc. Holding the telephone in her hand, she toyed with the idea, even going so far as to dial the first five digits of his number. Then she gently replaced the phone in its cradle. She had made the only reasonable decision. There would be no turning back.

Despite a slight warming trend over the weekend, the snowman was still there on Monday morning, looking as debonair as ever. Cathlyn stopped to stare at him for a long time. She knew she was going to miss him when he melted.

On her way into her office Cathlyn paused to finger the petals of the poinsettia plant on Shirley's desk. "You'd better water this," she reminded Shirley, "or it will fade and wilt. I saw one last Christmas that would have been beautiful, except no one had taken care of it." Memories of the pink sign for Dawn's Diner flashed on and off in her head, and unexpectedly she found her eyes brimming over. Quickly she disappeared into her office and prepared for her regular Monday morning patients.

"It's still too snowy for my daughter to visit," Mrs. Bixby explained as she trudged into Cathlyn's office in a pair of heavy boots. "And . . ." She stopped in the middle of the sentence, her faded blue eyes fixed on the large picture window behind Cathlyn's desk. "Oh, my," she exclaimed. "Oh, my!"

"Are you all right?" Cathlyn jumped out of her chair in alarm and put her hand on Mrs. Bixby's frail shoulder.

"I'm fine," Mrs. Bixby replied, "but just look out of your window. Oh, my," she repeated, shaking her white head from side to side.

Cathlyn turned and looked outside. After a moment she turned back to Mrs. Bixby. "There's nothing there," she said in bewilderment, wondering if the daughter had been right, after all. Perhaps poor Mrs. Bixby was having hallucinations.

"Just wait a minute," Mrs. Bixby promised patiently. "It will come back." She stood up and crossed the room to the window, with Cathlyn close behind her. "There, what did I tell you," she exclaimed, pointing to a small airplane in the distance. "You keep your eyes on that plane."

Cathlyn watched the azure sky in fascination as a silver plane banked to the right through some low clouds and then began to pass nearer the window.

"Do you see it?" Mrs. Bixby asked excitedly. "Do you see the banner?"

Cathlyn nodded, watching an outrageous red banner, three times the length of the plane, trailing behind in the wind. It looked like a dancing kite tail as it slowly pulled into clear view.

"Cathlyn: Come fly with me. Love, Marc." Mrs. Bixby read the words in a slow, deliberate voice. "There, I was sure that was what I saw," she cried out triumphantly. "That young man is a treasure."

"I guess so," Cathlyn responded weakly. She sank into her chair and watched in disbelief as the plane flew out over the lake, banked left, then turned to once again pass by her window. How long is this going to go on? she wondered.

"Here it comes again," Mrs. Bixby announced, her cheeks flushed. "I think we'll just skip the rest of my session today. I'm going outside for a better look at that plane—it's so exciting." She wriggled into her old muskrat coat and patted Cathlyn fondly on the arm. "Marry him," she advised. "I'll see you next week."

Cathlyn watched Mrs. Bixby's disappearing back, wondering for a moment just who was the psychologist. She saw the banner approach the window another time, turning away as Shirley appeared.

"Dr. Tate? Can you return a few phone calls between patients? The phone has been ringing off the hook—something about an airplane outside our building. . . ." Shirley's voice trailed off as the plane flew by. "'Cathlyn: Come Fly With Me. Love, Marc,'" she read aloud.

"I know what it says." Impatiently Cathlyn slammed her notebook down on her desk. "I can read too."

"Touchy, touchy," admonished Shirley. "May I assume you don't want to talk to the news reporter? He wants to know if you're the same Cathlyn the snowman belongs to and whether you know anything about an accident involving a squad car and a purple piano on Clark Street last month."

Cathlyn came angrily to her feet. "You tell that reporter—"

"No comment," Shirley said, finishing for her. "I already did."

"Fine," Cathlyn said. She began to pace back and forth across the carpet. The plane flew in front of the window again. "And close the blinds," she ordered her secretary.

"No," replied Shirley emphatically. "The blinds stay open."

"What do you mean, 'no'?" Cathlyn stopped pacing and stared at Shirley.

"Just what I said. No," Shirley repeated. "Mr. Thomas is your next patient. He has claustrophobia and always wants to sit facing the window. Do you want him to have a panic attack right in the middle of the session?"

"I suppose not," Cathlyn said wearily. Out of the corner of her eye she caught a glimpse of the shining silver plane again. "I'll sit with my back to the window," she declared, moving her chair around.

"You do that." Shirley broke into a big grin. "And let me know how it works out."

For the next three hours the plane flew back and forth every few minutes, as regularly as a metronome beating time. The patients were enthralled. Despite Cathlyn's repeated efforts to bring the discussion back to their problems, they were far more interested in the plane and the snowman, and what was going on between her and Marc. By the time she finally got home that evening, Cathlyn was exhausted. She judiciously avoided turning on the evening news on television. Instead, she picked up the phone and called Jean.

"You're no help," she complained to her friend when the only response she got was gales of laughter.

"I'm sorry." Jean giggled. "But I really do think it's funny. Marc is certainly imaginative. And, boy, is he persistent."

"I suppose so," Cathlyn muttered back.

"All the girls saw the plane on the evening news," Jean told her. "I have to be honest with you. They're rooting for Marc. Why don't you call him?"

"No," retorted Cathlyn. The question annoyed her. She'd expected Jean to understand. "How can you even suggest that, you of all people?" she demanded.

"And how can you, of all people, keep running away from this?" Jean challenged with characteristic frankness.

"I'm not running away—" Cathlyn asserted.

"Of course you are," Jean interrupted. "I don't blame you for being upset about the magazine article, but he probably didn't even know you when he did that interview. It can take six months or a year before a magazine article gets into print."

Cathlyn paused. Jean was right. She hadn't thought about that. "It doesn't make any difference," she answered finally. "He purposely didn't tell me about it—just like my father," she blurted out. At once she was both surprised and sorry she'd said it.

For a long moment Jean didn't respond. Then she said in careful tones, "Maybe you need to think that over, Cathlyn. Marc Harrison is nothing like your father. I'm afraid you're making a big mistake."

How can everyone except me be so damn sure I'm making a mistake? thought Cathlyn, hanging up the phone. She took a carton of cottage cheese from the refrigerator, removed the lid, and peered inside. Then, with disgust, she replaced the lid, shoved the container to the rear of the refrigerator, and stalked off toward the shower. At least the plane wouldn't be around forever, like that stupid snowman, she thought sourly.

Cathlyn soon discovered she was wrong. Every morning that week from nine to twelve, the plane cruised back and forth, clearly visible from her office window. The only thing that changed was the color of the banner. The first day it had been that outrageous shade of red. The second day it was flaming orange, the third electric blue, the fourth iridescent green. On Friday a trail of shocking pink graced the cold, gray winter sky. Cathlyn was very glad when the week was over.

But the weekend wasn't much better. By Sunday afternoon, after being confined to her apartment for two days by a blizzard, Cathlyn was tempted to phone Marc and tell him either to cut it out, or that she loved him, or both. Her mind was in a muddle. There simply weren't any answers. Marc's image haunted her day and night. When the Christmas carols poured out from her stereo, she didn't hear Perry Como singing "Silent Night." She heard Marc Harrison's rich baritone over the roar of a garbage truck. Jean's advice unsettled her. She really hadn't given Marc an opportunity to explain.

On Monday morning she pulled her little Toyota out of the garage onto the freshly plowed streets and snapped on the car radio to catch the traffic report from the police helicopter. Already cars were bumper-to-bumper, with every intersection in a snarl. Slowly Cathlyn's car crept along the slick side streets and eased out into the congestion on Michigan Avenue.

"Traffic is a mess this morning, folks," announced a cheerful voice through the static from the helicopter. "We're over the Dan Ryan Expressway right now. It's like looking at a parking lot with fender-benders everywhere. But the alternate routes don't look much better. Any drivers in that jam might as well take up knitting. Why don't you all stop honking and settle back while our favorite morning deejay spins some Christmas carols? We'll be back in just a few minutes with a look at the Outer Drive and a report on that tie-up on North Michigan Avenue."

"I Saw Mommy Kissing Santa Claus" blasted from the car speaker, and Cathlyn turned down the volume until the traffic report came back. While she was stopped in the long lines of cars, she idly glanced at the tiny twinkling lights on the trees along the parkway and then scanned the sky for the helicopter. In the distance, several blocks ahead, she could see it hovering against the dusky sky.

Cathlyn sighed and turned on her wipers to scrape the frost from her windshield. She looked impatiently at her watch, hoping she could make it to the office in time for her first patient. A bright orange Volkswagen honked loudly as it cut across two lanes of traffic and wormed in front of her. What is the problem this morning? Cathlyn wondered. She looked at her watch again. At this rate she'd be lucky to get to the office in time for lunch. The sun was coming up over the lake, bathing the tops of the skyscrapers in a deep orange glow. Cathlyn squinted, grateful for the enormous billboard on the top of a building just ahead that shielded her eyes from the bright rays.

"Folks," the helicopter reporter broke in, and Cathlyn turned up the volume. "Hold on to your hats and your horns. We've just located the source of the problem up on North Michigan Avenue, and you're never going to believe it."

"Get to the point," Cathlyn muttered, honking in frustration at a bus that spewed exhaust fumes at her.

"There's not an accident in sight down there—just one great big gaper's block. And you know what's causing it, folks? It seems Marc is wooing Cathlyn again, and this time he's rented one of the biggest billboards in town to advertise his love."

Cathlyn stared at the car radio. It wasn't possible. That wasn't really her name she had just heard.

"Cathlyn, if you're listening," the traffic reporter continued, "you'd make a lot of commuters happy if you'd marry Marc and change that billboard back to a beer ad."

Cathlyn took a deep breath and stretched over the dashboard to get a clear view. What she saw nearly made her collide with the car in front of her. The entire billboard had been painted Valentine red, and in the center was a gigantic, lacy white heart with an arrow piercing it. Written in flowing scroll across the heart was the simple schoolboy inscription, "Marc Loves Cathlyn."

She swerved sharply and slammed on her brakes. The billboard was a spectacle that made the snowman and the airplane look like also-rans. And the traffic reporter was correct. Even by Chicago standards, a gapers' block of major proportions had been created. Cathlyn had never seen Michigan Avenue like this. Cars were at a virtual standstill as drivers leaned out their windows to get a good look at the billboard. "I don't believe it," she said softly to herself. "I simply don't believe it."

When Cathlyn finally made it to the Hartford

Building, she pulled the collar of her coat up high around her face, hoping no one would recognize her in the lobby. She breathed a sigh of relief when the elevator doors closed. But she was less successful in slipping unnoticed past Shirley's desk.

"Good morning," chirped her secretary. "A bit late getting to work, aren't you?"

Cathlyn winced. No doubt Shirley already knew why. "A little bit late," Cathlyn agreed, hanging her coat carefully on the chrome rack and smoothing the collar. She sat down to remove her boots.

"I don't suppose it had anything to do with the new billboard on Michigan Avenue," Shirley suggested coyly.

"Possibly," Cathlyn answered.

"When the press calls, I should just tell them—"

"No comment," Cathlyn said. She breezed past Shirley with a bright smile and escaped to her inner office, closing the door behind her.

"Will you please marry that poor man?" Shirley called through the closed door. "Millions of people in the city of Chicago would be grateful."

Inside her office, Cathlyn stood silently staring out her window.

After a few minutes Shirley shouted through the closed door again. "It's good you won't answer me. That means you're thinking about it."

All right, Cathlyn admitted grudgingly to herself, *I'm thinking about it.*

She continued thinking about it. Day and

night for the next week, Marc rarely left her thoughts. She'd expected the feelings to subside as time passed, but, if anything, they were more intense than before. Every morning on the way to work she would look at the bright red billboard and read its inscription: "Marc Loves Cathlyn." She always smiled when she said the words. She missed him so much. Each day, when she walked into the Hartford Building, the snowman greeted her. He was getting gray from the city smog, and his smile had sagged slightly ever since one unseasonably warm day the week before. Maybe he's sad because . . . that's silly, she told herself.

Over the weekend Cathlyn called her sister to say she was going to stay in Chicago for Christmas. She just couldn't face a big celebration this year. Her sister would bustle around doing the last of the holiday baking, everyone would help trim the tree, the children would be wild with excitement. . . . Being alone for Christmas would be better than having to pretend to share joy she didn't feel, Cathlyn decided.

But when Jean stopped by on Saturday afternoon after finishing up the last of her Christmas shopping, she didn't agree. "You can't be all alone on Christmas," Jean protested. "I won't hear of it."

"I need to work some things out by myself," Cathlyn replied. "Remember how I used to say I had to get my head on straight? I need to be alone."

Jean swallowed the last bites of her muffin and stood up. She looked Cathlyn directly in the eye. "All you have to do is phone him," she said gently.

"I know." Cathlyn looked away, watching the thick cream make wavy rivulets in her coffee.

Christmas Eve brought a gentle snow that mantled the city like a fur cloak. Cathlyn put the shimmering star on the top of her apartment-size tree and stood back to admire her handiwork. The smell of cinnamon and cloves wafted from the kitchen. As Cathlyn fingered a plump gingerbread boy that dangled from a branch, she couldn't help but laugh at him. She wished Marc— Stop that, she thought, chiding herself. Marc isn't here and he isn't going to be. But he could be, she thought. The idea sent little chills of anticipation shooting through her. But, after all, she had made up her mind.

Sitting cross-legged on the floor, Cathlyn stuffed tissue paper back into the empty ornament boxes. What if she were making a big mistake? She was still angry about what Marc had done, but it was an anger tempered by time and shadowed by doubts about what might really be bothering her. In her mind, what Marc had done seemed to be all mixed up with what her father had done to her mother so many years before. Realistically that didn't make any sense.

Cathlyn stacked the ornament boxes in a neat, orderly pile. Marc must care about her, or he'd never have pursued her like he had. Not so doggedly, for so long. She'd wondered from the beginning whether there might be some explanation, but her resolve had been so fragile that she'd been afraid to see him or even talk to him. Cathlyn stood up and put the boxes away in the closet. She'd held out for a long time now, and she hadn't solved anything. Maybe it was time to quit running. Hesitantly she picked up the phone, then put it back down, unsure what she would say. What she said wasn't important, Cathlyn decided, as long as she called him. Picking up the phone again, she dialed Marc's number.

Her palms were clammy as she waited for it to ring—once, twice, three times. A feeling of emptiness stirred inside her. She counted the rings—five, ten, twenty—before she finally hung up the phone. She'd waited too long. Last Christmas Eve he'd been skiing, she remembered. Maybe he'd gone again. He had nothing to keep him here. Maybe he was at his parents'. It really didn't matter. Wherever he was, she wouldn't find him. She sank down into a chair and stared at the twinkling lights on the tree. Never in her life had she felt so lonely.

It was well after midnight when Cathlyn finally went to bed, and far into Christmas morning before she finally slept. But she still woke up early. Dawn found her sitting alone at her kitchen table drinking a cup of coffee. She jumped when she heard the pounding on the door. Her thoughts were only of Marc as she raced to open it. He had come, after all.

She threw back the heavy door, and then she stopped, numb with disappointment. "Merry Christmas!" the blue-uniformed messenger said, greeting her cheerily. She simply stared at him.

"A special-delivery letter for you, madam," he said, holding out a thin, cream-colored envelope. When she didn't respond, he thrust the envelope into her hands, and after shuffling his feet for a moment, he left. It wasn't until Cathlyn closed the door that she recognized Marc's handwriting.

Her hands trembling, she walked back into the living room and sat down on the couch. From somewhere in the distance she heard the strains of "White Christmas" playing on the radio. Carefully she turned the letter over, examining the embossed return address on the back. She gently ran the tip of her finger over the raised letters of Marc's name before she slit open the flap. Taking the letter from the envelope, Cathlyn began to read.

Christmas

Dearest Cathlyn,

I've tried every way I know to tell you how much I love you. But there are no words to describe love, just as there are no words to convey the agony of my loneliness since we've been apart.

I've spent so many evenings sitting in front of the window, looking out over the lights of the city, knowing that one of those lights is yours. I wonder sometimes what you're doing, and what you're thinking, and whether you hurt as much as I do. We lost something so precious. I can only hope that it isn't gone forever, because I can't face a future without you.

I know that you are more than justified in your decision. You trusted me, and I betrayed your trust. What I did was wrong, but I did it because I love you, and I need to explain what happened. Doing the interview was the price I paid for losing a poker bet. That was over a year ago—before we met. I tried to stop publication, and I thought the whole thing was over and forgotten, until the night of the art auction. I should have told you right then, but I put it off because I was desperately afraid I might lose you. The magazine article was even worse than I'd expected, but the real damage was what happened to us. I've done and said some things in my life that I'm not very proud of, but the writer of that article took them and twisted them and made them even worse. I don't want you to think of me that way.

I can't come to you, because you won't see me. And yet I ache to take you in my arms and hold you and tell you how very much I love you. I can't bear to lose you, Cathlyn. You mean more to me than anything else in my life.

I'm going to Angel House to spend Christmas Day, just as you did—or tried to do—a year ago. If you can find it in your heart to forgive, won't you come too?

I love you,

Marc

Cathlyn held the letter in her hands, her eyes filled with tears, her heart overflowing with love. He did have an explanation—she just hadn't been willing to listen. Her feelings had been all mixed up with so many things that happened so long ago. Cathlyn read the letter again. This was the real Marc Harrison, she realized. This was the man she had fallen in love with. He had tried every outlandish way he could think of to convince her that he loved her, from the gigantic snowman with his lopsided grin, to the garish flying banners, to the bright red Valentine billboard. But it wasn't until she had read this letter, simple and straight from his heart, that she was finally sure. He'd said it all when he wrote, "I did it because I love you." He had told her the truth in the best way he could.

Slowly Cathlyn stood up and walked over to her living room window, still holding Marc's letter. The sun was just coming up over the lake, its pale pink rays filtering softly through the thin layer of frosty ice on the glass. With the tip of her finger she traced the feathery patterns swirling across the window, thinking of Marc and how much she loved him. Just as he ached to take her in his arms, she longed to be there, safe and shielded, a part of him again.

She read the last paragraph of Marc's letter one more time. He would be at Angel House for Christmas, and if she could find it in her heart to forgive him . . . Forgive him? She was the one who needed to be forgiven. Cathlyn hugged the letter tight to her breast and laughed out loud, joyous peals of laughter that rang through the empty rooms. Suddenly she couldn't move fast enough.

By Christmas afternoon, clothes and shoes were scattered across her bed, flung on the back of her chair, and draped over her nightstand. Never in her life had Cathlyn had so much difficulty deciding what to wear. Nothing she owned seemed right.

Finally she dug in the back of her closet and discovered the red silk dress she had worn the Christmas before, the day she'd met Marc. A smile lit her face as she stroked the soft folds, remembering the sensations that had surged through her when his hand brushed her shoulder that very first night. She reached in her drawer for matching lingerie, slipped into the dress, and soon was fastening the backs of the delicate ruby earrings Marc had given her the previous summer. Finally she pulled on her coat, grabbed her purse in one hand and her guitar in the other. She had never been so excited.

A light snow was falling as Cathlyn drove along the quiet streets, thinking and remembering. A year was a very long time, yet it had flown past in a blur of happiness—until the last few weeks. Those had dragged endlessly. But today was Christmas—wonderful, beautiful Christmas. Cathlyn eased her car in between two drifts along the edge of Jean's snowy street, not even caring whether it got stuck.

"Merry Christmas," shouted a chorus of girls from the open front door of Angel House as Cathlyn made her way up the snow-packed walk.

"Merry Christmas." Cathlyn waved back, trembling with anticipation.

"We found your presents under the tree," Lisa told her, as Cathlyn stepped into the hallway.

"But we didn't open anything yet," Mandy assured her, as Cathlyn set down her guitar. "We were waiting for you."

"I'm so glad you're here," Jean exclaimed, giving Cathlyn a big hug.

"Me too," Cathlyn agreed. She hung her coat and purse on one of the few empty hooks, looking in vain for Marc's camel coat. "Is he here?" she whispered to Jean.

"Is who here?" her friend answered innocently.

"She's looking for her boyfriend, and he's not here," one of the girls said, teasing. Cathlyn was dismayed to feel the color rising in her cheeks. She never blushed.

"Hey, look, Cathlyn is turning the same color as her dress," called out another girl.

"Enough! Into the living room," ordered Jean. "Tommy, we need another eggnog."

Tommy appeared almost immediately, glass in hand. He gave Cathlyn a huge kiss on the cheek as he handed her the eggnog. "Our musician has arrived and we already have the angels—here's to the heavenly choir," Tommy joked. He raised his glass in a toast. "Now Christmas is complete."

Sipping her eggnog, Cathlyn followed them into the crowded living room. No, she thought to herself, it wasn't complete at all. Where was Marc? A fire was blazing in the fireplace, and everyone else had already gathered in the living room, which was a curious mixture of old and new. Pastel wallpaper had been hung, but the new furniture wouldn't be delivered for another month. With all the people and all the decorations, it didn't really matter. The room was bursting with noise and laughter. But without Marc it was empty.

Someone started a chorus of "Joy to the World," and everyone joined in. As they sang, Cathlyn looked at the Christmas tree, its soft lights twinkling near the front window. It was decorated entirely with angels, woven and carved and painted angels made by the girls, gold and silver angels received as presents, and, at the very top, the delicate crystal angel Cathlyn had given them the year before. The spirit of Christmas lived there, Cathlyn thought, not just that day but every day. The song ended, and her reverie ended with it, replaced by nagging doubts. Where was Marc? Was it possible he'd changed his mind and wouldn't come at all?

"How about some more eggnog?" Tommy asked, coming by with the pitcher.

"And have a Christmas cookie. I helped bake them," Mandy said proudly, holding out the plate. "But not too many before dinner," she added.

"Here, come sit by me," invited Lisa, scooching over so there was room for Cathlyn at the end of the lumpy couch.

As she sat down, Cathlyn heard a loud pounding on the front door, and a hush fell over the room. The pounding started again, but before anyone could move to answer it, the door burst open and in walked Santa Claus, a big brown bag slung over his shoulder. "Ho-ho-ho," he called out loudly, "and a Merry Christmas."

"Merry Christmas," the girls shouted back amid assorted giggles and cheers.

"Ho-ho-ho," Santa said again, and Cathlyn stared hard at him. He had come. Behind those voluminous white whiskers, under that funny red hat, it was Marc, his nose and cheeks bright red from the cold and his deep hazel eyes sparkling. He looked directly at Cathlyn, and for a long moment their eyes held each other. Warmth and happiness washed over her, and suddenly Christmas was complete.

As the room quieted, Marc looked away. "Now let's see what we have here," he said jovially, dropping his overflowing bag to the floor under the archway.

Cathlyn watched him distribute the presents, calling each girl by name, saying something special to her, and wishing her a Merry Christmas. How could I have been so right, and so blind, I didn't even recognize it? Cathlyn asked herself. *How could I ever have doubted him?*

Marc worked his way around the room, saving Tommy for last. "For you I have something you've wanted for years," Marc said, grinning. Cathlyn stood up on tiptoe to see better. From the bottom of the bag he pulled out a large wooden sign, richly embossed. Carved into the center were the words MEN'S ROOM. The girls convulsed in laughter.

In the ensuing confusion Marc made his way

across the room to Cathlyn. "And now for the most special angel," he whispered to her. He reached deep into the pocket of his furry red pants. Then, taking her hand in his, he slipped a dazzling diamond solitaire set in gold on her ring finger. "Will you marry me?" he whispered into her hair.

"Oh, yes, Marc, yes," she said, throwing her arms around his neck. "I was wrong . . . I'm so sorry . . ." He held her close, his lips finding hers, gently, tenderly, in a declaration of love. They parted, suddenly aware of the silence all around them.

"Hey, look," said a voice. "Cathlyn's kissing Santa Claus."

"All right!" called another. "She and Marc finally got it together."

"Quick, get the mistletoe," yelled still another, and everybody cheered.

Jean came up and hugged them both. "It's about time," she said, and then she saw the ring. "Wow!" she exclaimed. "You've done it!" And she hugged them again.

"Dinner's on," she shouted over the noise, then turned back to Marc and Cathlyn. "Tommy's carving the turkey. You can make a general announcement during dessert."

Cathlyn started to follow Jean, but Marc stopped her. "Jean, I'm sorry," he said, "but we can't join you for dinner this year."

"We can't?" Cathlyn looked up at him in surprise.

"No," he said, his eyes twinkling. "I'm afraid we have reservations somewhere else."

"I'm sorry," Jean said, "but I understand. Why don't you go right now, quietly, and you won't have to explain."

"Thanks," Cathlyn said to her friend.

As Jean turned toward the dining room to join Tom and the girls, Marc quickly slipped out of his Santa costume. He helped Cathlyn with her coat, and they hurried out the front door. Once on the porch, he wrapped her in his arms and kissed her again, a deep, burning kiss. "Oh, Marc, I love you," Cathlyn breathed, "for always and always I'll love you. And the ring . . ." She looked down at her finger where the brilliant diamond sparkled fire in the sunlight. "It's lovely, Marc," she said softly.

"Not half as lovely as you," he answered, slipping his arm around her waist and guiding her toward the car.

"There's so much I need to explain—" he began.

"No, Marc," Cathlyn said, stopping him. "You don't have to explain anything. I got all mixed up with a lot of feelings from a long time ago, feelings that had nothing to do with you, or us. It was when I read your letter that I finally understood."

Marc took her in his arms again. "I do love you, Cathlyn, more than I ever realized it was possible to love someone. I guess we've both worked some things out."

"I know we have," Cathlyn agreed.

"Just one request," he added, looking deep into her eyes. "Next time we have any working out to do, let's do it together."

Cathlyn smiled and nodded before his lips found hers, sealing a promise each could finally make to the other.

"And now, my love," he said, opening the car door, "we need to get going."

"Where?" Cathlyn asked, looking puzzled. "From what your letter said, I thought we were going to have dinner here."

Marc grinned at her with a wicked twinkle in his eye. "We could have," he answered, "except that we have reservations elsewhere."

"But where?" Cathlyn asked.

"Dawn's Diner, of course," he replied, and together they burst into laughter that rang all the way down the snow-covered street.

About the Author

Virginia-based authors Sally Siddon and Barbara Bradford formed their dynamic writing team several years ago and have been creating best-selling romances ever since. Their heroines are supercharged and vivacious, their heroes as breathtaking as the worlds they conquer, and the combination will enthrall readers everywhere. Sally's and Barbara's hobbies include reading, sewing, gardening, camping, and relaxing at the beach as well as raising teenage sons and daughters. With such involved lifestyles, it's easy to see why they can create the perfect escape through their novels!